ACKNOWLEDGMENTS

One-hundred-forty-three entries poured in from 110 FWA members, thirty-three of whom submitted two stories. Entries were posted without author names to a specially designed website accessible only by judges. Our judges read and scored the entries. FWA is deeply indebted to them, and thanks each for their time, dedication, and expertise.

Each entry is presented as submitted, with only minor editing, if mistakes like missing quote marks, misspelled words, or forgotten periods happen to be caught during the audit stage. Many of the entrants took advantage of either attending one of FWA's many Critique Groups across the state or using FWA's editing service, which offered special pricing. The quality of entries reflects the professionalism and growth of our members. Thank you, Bobbie Christmas, for managing that special editing service.

Thank you to Charles H. Cornell for the design of the cover for our 12th Collection volume: *Florida Writers Association Collection, Volume 12, Create an Illusion.*

It is with heartfelt gratitude that FWA acknowledges Mark Newhouse's contribution to this publication. He had perhaps the hardest job of all – picking only ten entries to be his favorites out of the sixty winning stories.

The seventh annual Youth Writers Collection Contest, created to provide our youth members an opportunity to become published authors, produced 11 winners from 19 authors who submitted entries. FWA acknowledges and thanks our Youth Writers Groups, their Group Leaders and especially Mark H. Newhouse, Kristen Stieffel, and Wanda Luthman for their efforts to accomplish this goal.

Our sincere thanks from FWA's Board of Directors to Antonio Simon, Jr. of Darkwater Syndicate for being our official Collections publisher, and for graciously donating all publishing costs. His patience and expertise throughout all aspects of production were invaluable.

Su Gerheim

Collection Contests Coordinator, 2020

TABLE OF CONTENTS

Create An Illusion
Florida Writers Association Youth Collection, Vol. 7

Age Group 9-13

Age Group 14-17

INTRODUCTION

CREATE AN ILLUSION

FLORIDA WRITERS ASSOCIATION COLLECTION, VOL. 12

I'm grateful *The Devil's Bookkeepers*, set in the Holocaust ghetto my parents miraculously survived, won Best Published Book of the Year, and Gold Medal Historical Fiction, in the RPLA. It is ironic that I completed the last volume of this trilogy shortly before mankind got our illusion shattered that we are masters of the universe by a virus, one of Earth's tiniest residents. (Remember H.G. Welles?) As writers, we hope to create illusions people believe, ones that resonate with family and the future. I never visited the Lodz ghetto, but am thrilled when readers report they feel as if they trudged every muddy path and choked as the noose tightens on the souls lost there. Getting readers to care is what the writer-illusionist does, and these winning entries do just that.

First, a ride on the "Okefenokee" reveals its secret. Next, we race to a hospital on a chilly night in "It's Time." A son confronts the memory of a cruel father in "A Good Man." "Chosen" takes us soaring into a mystical ritual. A girl believes she is invisible in "A Shrouded Forest." "Mable's Fight" pits a woman against an unusual adversary. "The Graying" offers a glimpse of the future, or present, as a woman shops for essentials. "The Safe Tree," and Yellow Leaf in a Puddle," ask if safety is only an illusion. In "Cancelled," we attend an apartment sale with a twist. These are only the Top Ten of more than sixty entries from some of Florida's best writers.

When Don Quixote sees himself in a mirror, his illusion shatters. This year many of our illusions were shattered by a disease that turned life into a sci-fi novel. One illusion we mustn't lose is our belief that we can defeat the evil 'windmills' of this world. It is therefore exciting to see the works of the Florida Writers Association Youth featured with adult winners. If anyone can right the wrongs of this world, it is our young. And that is not an illusion.

Paraphrasing Rod Serling, "You are entering another dimension… the world of illusions." And what a world it is!

Mark Newhouse, 2020

The Illusion

"The girl's empty eye sockets stared up at her as if they knew what she was contemplating. Smash the hammer down; the illusion would be preserved.

Dr. Leslie Crown gazed at the trees surrounding the dig. They were conspicuously shorter than the forest that had concealed the abandoned colony for three centuries. Dr. Rayburn Stanton, her mentor, had scoured the few colonists' journals, and after years of searching for the 'needle in the haystack,' found the peninsula the diarists described as hell.

An icy wind reminded Leslie of the cruelty of the coastal winters. She thought of the townspeople nestled in their refurbished church, proud of their history now that the town had become a tourist mecca. Many residents dressed in period clothing to enhance the experience. "How can I let you destroy all that?" She raised the hammer over the skull.

The grad students would arrive soon, working even on a Sunday. Months of digging with child-sized spades, brushing off centuries of encrusted sediment and rock, was exhausting. They were spurred on by the hope of finding any clue to the site's mysterious history. "Some histories are best lost," Leslie said to the skull.

Heroes Landing, as it was renamed by the town council, boasted a new museum, a tribute to the first explorers. The on-going restoration and the museum were co-funded by the university and state. Leslie, a forensic archeologist, was eager to see her name engraved with Stanton's. The skull, even with the bottom half missing, assured that. But at what price?

Leslie held the skull up against the blue sky, tilting it, so the wintery clouds were visible through the unnatural opening where the brain would have been. Her measurements convinced her the child's head wasn't cracked open by an Indian ax or by a rock. More likely, the hole was caused by one blow of a pike, a weapon used by English knights. She turned the skull over.

"Still there," she said, running her finger down the white surface, her fingernail being stopped at each striation.

Leslie glanced at the posts that marked the site where the first church stood. Through the partly restored rock wall, her eyes focused on three crosses erected by Stanton's team to mark where three early settlers were exhumed five years earlier. After tentative identification, the skeletons were enshrined in glass cases. Brass plaques detailed the courageous exploits of Captain James Walker, John Bedloe, a priest, and Samuel Amos Ramsdale, a colony leader. All were considered saviors of the colony that was almost destroyed by the winter of 1609-1610. The arrow and spearheads found in the digs attested to hostilities the new settlers also faced. Of the four hundred souls listed in the original manifests, only forty-two were left alive after that ferocious winter. Streets and schools were named after these founders. Monuments to the brave men and few women who miraculously survived were erected after widely publicized fund-raising campaigns.

When Leslie was recruited, Stanton boasted, "You'll share the glory." But now she knew something Stanton never suspected. None of them did.

At first, Leslie was excited to find what appeared to be a mother lode of pottery and rusted implements. Digging deeper, she uncovered bones from various animals. Examining them, she detected striations in some of the bones and some teeth marks, some from animals, others human. The specimens, cataloged and photographed, were sent to the university lab where teeth marks were measured and DNA, if any, extracted, classified, and stored. Exceptional care was taken to avoid contamination.

Stanton was excited. Leslie, he theorized, had discovered a trash pile, an invaluable source of clues as to how settlers used tools and their eating habits. "It's truly a case of one man's trash is another's treasure. This stash of discards could be our most significant discovery in learning what happened to these early settlers."

Stanton declared the roped-off square her realm. Leslie saw it as her claim to fame. Others could only envy her as she dug up more bits of pottery, metal, and a variety of animal bones. A book, The Starving Time, co-authored with Stanton, promised to cement her reputation and affirm the history of the miraculous survival of the early colonists.

Slash marks made by the downward motion of dull knives were evidence of the shearing of meat from various animal bones. The lab determined that some bones were from dogs. The colonists were desperate, Leslie reasoned. Other bone fragments revealed the settlers had been forced to eat rats. Being a scientist, she was able to rationalize for herself that starvation had forced the suffering colonists to search for sustenance anywhere available. Evidence of their desperation added to the heroic narrative. And then she found the skull.

The sound of a motor. The bus.

Leslie gripped the hammer.

A door slammed. The next crew of diggers was ready to seek their own buried treasure.

The skull. It had been found buried among the bones of slaughtered animals, a human skull, a young girl. Struck dead by a heavy blow that cracked her head wide open, the girl dropped to the ground. Did she know what was going to happen? Who was she? How was she chosen? There were striations along both sides of what would have been her face. They were approximately five to six inches in length and ran like waves down the surface. Leslie let her finger follow the trail of slicing cuts that ran from under the left eye down to the top of what remained of the girl's lower jaw. Thankfully, there weren't any teeth marks, but the tell-tale striations shocked her when she first noticed them. Closer examination revealed the knife trails were the same as found on the animal bones, the implication, a nightmare.

A few blows of the hammer would erase this threat to the heroic saga of the brave and righteous colonists.

Seconds left.

No one else had seen the skull. Stanton didn't know about it yet. It was Leslie's discovery. Hers alone. She imagined the horror the girl must have felt, her starving family and friends surrounding her like ravenous wolves. She felt the girl's terror as the weapon raised over her eyes. When it struck, the girl dropped to the ground and then…

The image of the young girl's body being savaged by a knife...

It will shatter everything they believe about their ancestors, Leslie thought. It will destroy the myth, the bedrock of their faith, their pride. She lifted the hammer.

The wind interrupted. In the chill, Leslie heard Stanton's voice, "Congratulations! Imagine how this true horror story will bring crowds to our discovery. We'll all be famous and rich." But it will destroy their illusions, she thought.

The hollowed-out eyes stared at the ceiling lights through the top of the glass case. Leslie held up a plastic replica for a busload of tourists. "These striations are from the knife slicing off her flesh," she announced into the microphone as the tourists switched their cameras to close-up lenses so everyone could see the gashes in the girl's skull."

Mark Newhouse

Mark H. Newhouse is grateful his novel, *The Devil's Bookkeepers 1*, about the Holocaust ghetto his parents miraculously survived, won the Gold Medal Historical Fiction and Best Published Book of the Year in the Royal Palm Literary Awards. A Retired NY teacher, he is Florida Writers Association Youth Chairperson, and an FWA Director.

MARK NEWHOUSE'S
TOP TEN PICKS

OKEFENOKEE

Mud-born
the mythical beast
rises—
sole,
secretive,
it rattles in its armor.
Groans   wide.
Inviting in
the fleeing moon.

In the trees
Spanish moss
catches at the echoes
of a breeze—
delicate,
deceitful,
it is not   dependent.
An unreliable guide.

And that leaf—
hooded,
hiding
the treacherous tunnel.
The sticky   pitcher,
a meat-eater
plying ancient enchantments.
Luring the innocent.

The Okefenokee
is full of artifice—
the waterways illusory
as sphagnum islands
pop   up
close channels,
bedevil swampers.

Those who go there
follow the flicker
of the moon through the trees.
Some never find home.

Shutta Crum

Shutta Crum's poems have appeared in many journals including Ann Arbor (W)rites, ArtAscent, Typehouse, Stoneboat, and soon in Main Street Rag. Her chapbook *When You Get Here* came out in 2020. She has several children's books out; published by major publishers. She is an oft-requested instructor and speaker. www.shutta.com.

MARK NEWHOUSE'S
TOP TEN PICKS

It's Time

"It's time," my wife said, nudging me gently in the ribs. "We need to go."

I rubbed the sleep from my eyes and looked at my watch—three-thirty on Christmas morning. "Are you sure? The doctor said—"

"I'm sure."

Stepping into my sweats, fully awake now, I considered the sixty-mile trip to the hospital. At this hour the traffic shouldn't be bad. "Have you got everything?"

She nodded, and I could see the pain in her reddened eyes as she struggled to stand, the added weight she carried hindering her slightly.

"It'll be all right. Do you need help to the car?"

"No, I'm okay. Just get the door."

"Hang on. Let me warm it up first." I pulled on a hoodie, grabbed the keys, and hustled out. I should've taken a moment to put slippers on. My bare feet screamed when I stepped on the frozen ground. I hesitated, looking to where the car sat twenty-feet away, and back to the inviting golden glow of the foyer. Ah, screw it. I ran to the car, forced the key past the ice covering the lock, opened the door, and jumped in. "Shit, it's cold."

Mercifully, the car started—new battery. I turned the heat knob to the right and cranked the fan to max. I kept my hands in my armpits and waited as the defroster began to melt the windshield ice. Satisfied the old Buick would not stall, I steeled myself for the return sprint to the front porch across the slippery flagstones of the walkway.

My wife stood in the foyer as I burst through the door. Her sober demeanor banished the curt comments I was preparing to share regarding the timeliness of the latest cold front, and I moved past her to retrieve my shoes and jacket. I needed more than my thin hoodie.

"Watch your step. The ground is icy." I held her close to my side as we worked our way to the car.

It took a moment to lower her in the passenger seat but finally had her buckled in. I shut the door, ran back to double-check I locked the front door, and realized the keys were in the Buick's ignition.

"Damn." I rushed back, apologized for the gust of cold as I snatched the keys, then ran back up the steps to secure the deadbolt.

My ears and cheeks stinging, I dropped into the driver seat. Jerking the car door closed, I said a silent prayer. I slid the key in the ignition and turned it, hoping. The engine turned, coughed once, and started. I released the breath I had not realized I was holding.

I reached over and squeezed my wife's cold hand. "You okay?"

She turned wet eyes to me but did not speak.

"Yeah, I know." I put the Buick in gear and backed out of the driveway.

I twisted the wiper control to low. The rhythmic scratch, thump of the blades as they scraped slush from the windshield, sounded very loud over the silence in the cabin.

The radio remained off. Up here in the mountains static was the only guarantee.

I said nothing. What was there to say? I knew we both understood what was happening. I certainly didn't want to open a dialogue about it. I knew the consequences should I broach the subject. I had been here several times before.

But, it was a responsibility, one I took seriously, and it was time.

Neither of us said a word for over an hour.

I turned in the entrance of the empty hospital parking lot and felt the tires crunch over snow and ice as I steered the Buick into a spot close to the doors. Pale yellow light spilled from windows onto the latest snowpack, and I thought of Frank Zappa.

"Don't eat the yellow snow." The words were out before I realized what I said. "I'm sorry — poor timing. I'm just…God, I hate this."

My wife touched my arm as I opened the door. "She needs you to be strong."

I stopped, my left hand on the door handle, my right still gripping the wheel. "I will be. I always am." I climbed out, pushed the door shut, and stared at the illuminated sign over the sliding doors of the hospital: Blue Pearl Animal Hospital.

Sighing, I went to the passenger door and opened it. "Give her to me." I gently extricated the small wrapped bundle from my wife's embrace. "Wait here. I'll take care of it. If you get cold, the keys are in the ignition."

Choked sobs were her only response. I eased her door shut and turned toward the light of the emergency entrance.

A veterinary assistant met me at the check-in desk. "Good morning, sir. Is that Abigail?"

I nodded. My vision blurred as tears formed. I blinked them away and took a deep breath. Lifting the nine-year-old Scottish Terrier higher in my arms, I said, "It's time."

Ricky Keck

Mr. Keck has been writing fiction for thirty years and has six self-published titles and several short stories to his credit. He lives in the Tampa Bay area with his wife and two Scottish Terriers.

MARK NEWHOUSE'S TOP TEN PICKS

A Good Man

Every time I went near that door, I would get the belt from my father. Frankly the sharp sting of his anger wounded me more than that piece of leather, and I knew in our little household of three that Papa's orders were to be obeyed. Mama, the lump of sugar in father's bitter coffee, ran interference for me, but we both knew his number one rule was to keep away from that tiny room at the end of the upstairs hallway. There was something behind that door that he wouldn't talk about. It was a riddle I itched to solve and at eleven I felt confident I was clever enough to outsmart him, an old man of nearly forty.

My mother often told me that my Papa was a good man, but I struggled to see it in the distant and preoccupied person who walked around with slumped shoulders as if carrying a troublesome burden. As the neighborhood baker, Papa was not wealthy but he managed to keep his house in a state that neighbors envied and our home was always filled with the mouth-watering aroma of yeasty warm bread and vanilla cakes.

Knowing father was a sound sleeper, I often tiptoed to the forbidden end of the long hallway, my feet barely registering the cold of the wooden planks that Mama kept so polished. I would stand before the mystery door willing my pounding heartbeat to slow so I could better hear. Was that a creak? A muffled cough? Occasionally I would be brave enough to lie on the floor and peek under, but I never saw anything.

The little scratching noises were just some rats my mom told me. With a cracked voice and a tight fist held to her mouth she warned me to never mention it to my father or anyone else. But rats don't light candles whose yellow light seeped out from under the door and spilled onto my toes. "Who's there," I would whisper, and the candle would go out. Rats don't blow out candles either.

I found it curious that the doorknob had been removed and it, along with the keyhole, had been filled in with putty. Sometimes I would peer up at the room from the outside of the house. Or at least where the room would be, as there was no window.

One day I came home from school and heard my parents upstairs by the forbidden door. Quietly climbing the stairs and peering through the banister I could see my mother dabbing her eyes and papa leaning heavily against the wall with both hands on top of his bowed head.

The words came out even though I tried to stop them. "What's wrong?"

Papa snapped his gaze in my direction and to this day I'll never forget the frightened look on his face. I scurried backwards, tripped over my feet, and tumbled down the stairs bouncing hard on the landing. My alarmed mother's cry turned to relief as I picked myself up and ran.

"You will never speak of this again," Papa roared to my back as I headed towards the basement to hide among the flour sacks and sugar barrels

The next day when I came home from school the door was gone. Papa had covered it with plaster and the wall now sported brightly flowered wall paper. Mama lined both sides of the hallway with old trunks from the attic. When he was satisfied, Papa closed the door, to our new storage area, locked it, and pocketed the key. Mama stuffed rags under the door claiming there was a draft. I never saw that door opened again.

After that I stopped trying to solve the riddle. Papa busied himself baking soft bread and sweet pastries for the many soldiers that came into town and never seemed to leave. The years passed and I forgot about the door. I left for college in Amsterdam, and finally left the town for good. My parents lived a quiet life and passed away at a nice old age. I didn't think about the mysterious door again until I inherited the house. Now I stood in front of the fading wallpaper, a crow bar in my sweaty hand, my father's warnings ringing in my brain. But I was not eleven any more.

Even though I was now in my seventies I had no problem tearing through the brittle covering of plaster that disguised the entrance to the room. The edge of the door came open with a pop of suction and a sprinkle of white paste particles. I switched on my flashlight with shaky hands and peered into the darkness. At first glance it appeared the room was empty. There was no furniture, no bookshelves, no rugs. Disappointment brought a frown to my face and I let out a defeated whoosh of air at the likelihood that I would never discover this room's secret. I scanned the light to the left and caught a square shape on the floor under a pile of cobwebs. Squatting down with knees that now complained, I found a dusty book. *Papa hid a book?* It wasn't forbidden to read in Holland back in those days. In fact, I had had many books. I settled on the floor and opened the cover of the book that had gotten me into so much trouble in my youth and the reason for a good many restless nights. The pages expectedly were faded and the edges dry. The corners crumbled as I handled them. The musty smell of aged paper and ink hit my nose, the kind of ink that came from an inkwell, bold and black at one time, but now brown and faded. It seemed to be a journal, a list of names and dates, some in my father's wobbly handwriting. There were eight pages in all, twenty names on each page. The last three entries were: Anne Berman, in April 14, 1942, out May 2, 1943; Micha Schwarz, in June 6, 1943, out June 20, 1943; Sol Spelman, in July 2, 1944. There was no second date on this name.

I rested my back on the wall puzzling at what I had found. How had it gotten there? How had my father become the owner? What would it have done to this family if the Nazis had found it? My father's fear found my heart. My flashlight fell from my hand as I pondered these questions, and the beam rolled around the tiny room. And there tucked in the corner I saw him. The skeleton of a man. I knew it was a man from his shirt and trousers. And the yellow star hand-stitched on his pocket.

Now the plastering, wallpapering, and rags under the door made sense. Along with my mother's profound sadness, and my father's tired face pondering dangers I could never imagine. I pledged that I would enter an end date in the journal for Sol, the man I whispered to, the man who never made it out of our tiny room at the end of the hallway like all those before him

My mother had been right. Papa had been a good man.

Jody Lebel

A criminal court reporter by day, Jody Lebel writes in the romantic suspense genre. Dozens of her short stories have sold to Woman's World magazine and Chicken Soup for the Soul. Raised in charming New England, she now lives with her two cats in southern Florida.

MARK NEWHOUSE'S TOP TEN PICKS

CHOSEN

Prologue

In the dim mist of times past, the woodland spirits favored Canyon's Edge Village with a Staff of Fire and a Blade of Protection to prevent warring tribes from taking the land and enslaving the people.

The spirits chose two villagers, known as the Guardian and the Knife, to wield the talismans of Staff and Blade. After fifty years they were to identify their successors and train them from birth.

Succession was conditioned upon a challenge, however. The two had to survive a leap into the Deep Canyon. One could not succeed without the other. Should either fail, both would die, the talismans would be stripped of their power, and the village would be overrun.

***

The Challenge as Recounted by Golden Eagle

I endured the freezing night alone and nestled in a bower of pine needles. The Sky Warrior constellation tracked her nightlong arc befriending me between my fleeting moments of nightmare-filled slumber. At first light to a crescendo of birdsong, she faded and left me to make my own way.

Rising with the sun, I clad myself in ceremonial garb–beaver skin pounded to its thinnest, oiled to a slick sheen, and emblazoned with a mighty eagle.

I lifted my head high and decamped to Canyon's Edge Stream. The rocky red path drew me forward. I stumbled, ripped from reverie I barely avoided clumps of crimson cactus. Burbling waters then lifted my spirit and urged me on.

The ancient gnarled pine dividing stream and trail marked the village edge. Kneeling before the sinewy giant, I begged the forest gods and canyon sprites, "Ease my fears; give me the courage to make the leap. Embolden my companion and sharpen her blade. Lift us then on wings of renewal and hope."

Winding through deerskin tents and romping children, I approached the Bird-of-Prey Lodge. There the Elders encircled the black stone pit containing the morning fire.

The circle opened, revealing Sparrowhawk, my companion for our years of preparation. Behind her, flames blasted sparks and smoke skyward. Just beyond lay Deep Canyon, dropping twenty thousand feet into a yawning gorge.

Sparrowhawk's green eyes felt like they pierced mine. I unveiled my best warrior face, while silently offering a prayer of supplication. *Dear gods, deliver us from death. Raise us up to protect the village.*

We sat among the Elders and ate a sparse meal. Assaulted by wind-driven gusts of fire smoke, our eyes burned and watered. Engrossed in breakfasting, I almost missed Sparrowhawk's signal. She nodded, shifting her gaze to the villagers' grave faces laden with worry and fear.

The meal completed, the chant began, "She comes; she sees; she guides." Over and over, voices rose, and the call went out. From the deerskin village and the rock caves, the tribe gathered.

The Elders, shunning the intensity of glowing black stone and billowing smoke, retreated into the throng. High above, a ring of fire blossomed and encircled dark clouds. With a sun in the center it appeared as a target in the sky.

A clap of thunder was followed by the thumping of mighty wings. The target melted, morphed, and descended. The Guardian stood opposite us through roaring flames. Her speckled wings were spread wide and a blazing orb topped her staff. I barely noticed the Knife at her side brandishing a gleaming blade across his chest.

She addressed the tribe. "As it has been for a thousand years, the Guardian shall patrol the sky on tireless wings and the Knife shall gather the brave and strong to defend the village. We stand before you this day to witness the test of succession. It shall begin when the sun reaches its zenith." Her attention came to rest on Sparrowhawk and me. "If you survive, the Staff of Fire and the Blade of Protection shall be passed to you, the Chosen."

We sat cross-legged in silence for the intervening hours, contemplating the learnings from honing body, mind, and spirit to face the challenge.

At high noon we moved to the chasm. When I turned to Sparrowhawk, the hint of her smile sent my heart leaping. Fear subsided.

Emerging from a lone cloud, the sun spilled scorching beams. We took in the villagers arrayed behind us and then turned to face the Guardian hovering over Deep Canyon with her staff held high. She stiffened, nodded to us–and lowered her staff. We slingshot forward, reaching our maximum velocity and catapulted over the ledge.

The updraft lifted me to the blue sky, and then I plummeted into the gorge. Building speed, feeling fear running from mouth to gut, I rolled and tumbled. Sparrowhawk spun close by; we raced to the boulders far below.

Sharp spires and cliff-clinging trees whizzed by. I shifted my body as I was trained. Stabilized, I sensed her nearby.

My ears throbbed, popping again and again. Turbulent winds tore at us as we plunged. I caught a glimpse of Sparrowhawk; she clutched a burnished blade flashing in the sunshine. With her free hand she reached for me and missed, ripped away by a powerful gust. She adjusted, both arms freed to maneuver; the blade between her teeth and blood on her lips. She rotated, flared, and slowed, moving up and out of sight. The valley floor resolved into a narrow river.

I jerked; Sparrowhawk's feet jabbed at my ribs, her nails tore at my back. Finally, her legs wrapped around my waist.

The first hack dug deep into the blade of my shoulder. The second jab of her knife sent me spasming as rapid slashes ripped flesh from my back. Taking her time yet wasting none, Sparrowhawk completed her task, unwrapped her legs, and pushed me away.

This was the moment. I pulled my arms and elbows in tight. Hugging myself, I broadened my shoulders, extending backbone, tendons, and neck. My training took over, and I tapped into instinct. Wrenching, I unfurled from my back's open gashes one appendage and then another. The rush of air separated and dried golden feathers as rhythmic flexion engaged my flight.

I swooped to Sparrowhawk, grabbed her, and pulled up in a violent motion. Saved from plummeting into the river, joined in flight, we darted across the rippling blue waters shaded from the burning suns by my golden expanse of wings. Reaching the sunbaked rocky shore, we were thrust upward.

Minutes later we flew above the village. It had survived for untold generations, and we had secured it for one more.

The Guardian joined us, and together we descended to the black stone pit. Laying the staff and blade before the Elders, she took the Knife's hand. The succession completed, they ascended, moved out over Deep Canyon, and faded from view, never to return.

My energy depleted, I barely noticed the rising chorus as I fell to my knees, placed my head on the ground, and gave thanks to the gods.

Sparrowhawk leaned in as her lips brushed my ear. "The village prepares the feast. The Elders will stand our guard until the sun sets and rises once more."

"What does the tribe chant?"

She pulled me closer. Our eyes locked. “They chant that you are the Guardian, and I am The Knife.”

Mike Summers

Mike had a scientist dad and played with lots of dangerous stuff, like rocket fuel and dynamite. His professional life was spent in Silicon Valley while also traveling the world innovating at advanced technology laboratories. Mike is finally getting to write about the ideas and worlds he’s seen and imagined.

MARK NEWHOUSE'S TOP TEN PICKS

A SHROUDED FOREST

Masha left the camp through the front gate under the noses of the SS, a feat never imagined by any prisoner, much less the timid Masha. For months after, she hid in plain sight undetected, crediting God for bestowing her with the gift of camouflage along with its consequent defect of forgetfulness.

Early in captivity, she began to blend into her surroundings, unnoticed by anyone. Her friends failed to see her in their midst even when she sat beside them. At roll call, they cast frantic eyes about for her, fearing the entire block would suffer if Masha failed to appear. Then, where moments ago there was only emptiness, she'd suddenly materialize. Unable to fully control the episodes, she was relieved to go unnoticed by her captors at inauspicious moments.

Naturally, the prison uniforms, so thin and faded, assisted the invisibility, as did her general degree of starvation. The wind blew through her as did the snow and rain. If her work assignment was the sewing room, she became the color of the fabrics she cut. In the machine shop, she took on the luster of metal. That day, when the guards took turns shooting inmates behind the fence, distracting themselves and leaving the gate ajar, so absorbed were they in their target practice, Masha sauntered out, not as quickly as her bladder urged, but as though bringing up the rear of yet another work detail. She expected to be shot or beaten, so when she reached the woods unharmed, she collapsed in relief, wept, and praised God, only to remember belatedly the life she left behind in the camp.

Thereby compelled to remain close for months after her escape, she eluded several hunting parties; once, by hiding inside a tree so cavernous, not even their torches betrayed her. Other times, she slipped soundlessly from one canopy of birch to another, confusing the hounds beneath her, so that the guards soon gave up the tail. She learned to step lightly, so her footprints dissolved as soon as she left them.

From a tree just beyond the guards' barracks, she monitored her younger brother, Avi, long the paramour of a certain guard, who stroked the child as he might a pet. Avi was all the family she had left, so she yearned to tuck him beneath her mantle of invisibility, waving and willing him to recognize her, though by then, she would not have recognized herself. Without ever seeing her own reflection, she knew that, like the other prisoners, her eyes were sunken, her lips grown thin and her cheeks hollow. She managed to escape the regular blows given by the guards at the cost of losing her brother and the past they'd known together.

"Come," she whispered, willing Avi to discern her outline within the branches, but the boy only looked on blankly.

When the guards departed the camp, marching out all the able-bodied prisoners, Masha reentered it, searching for Avi in the sickbay, where the seriously ill were improbably left alive. They made stone soup to nourish those who weren't already dead. She foraged the barracks for potatoes or a stray vegetable. Asking every survivor about Avi, she realized that, like her, the adolescent had simply vanished.

On the fourth day, she found her former bunkmate, Dora, alive and coughing by the electrified gate from which Masha made her escape. They embraced one another.

Then Dora scolded her, "Where have you been these past four days? I've looked all over fearing you'd fallen or perhaps somehow you once again had blended into the dust."

Masha shook her head, "That wasn't me. I left by the gate months ago, staying in the forest only to watch over Avi who remained behind. Has anyone seen him?"

Dora gave her a confused gesture but spoke tenderly, "Don't you remember, Avi died months ago? The guard, the one who was always with him, made him run along the fence before shooting him. We both saw it happen, standing on this very spot."

Flames flashed at the back of Masha's memory, and the roar of guards' laughter as they matched one another's shooting skills spilled over her in icy sheets, taking her breath and voice. Finally, she murmured, "The forest was so real."

While Masha continued to remember Avi as from a high branch overlooking the guards' quarters, still fondled and caressed as he stared into the forest beyond her, the desperate glance that passed between them only moments before his young body exploded never ceased to propel her into further flights of time and space. On the streets and shops of a new home and homeland, his face flickered at her as the whole and cheerful boy she knew when they were young, yet those images came only fleetingly and for precisely the same amount of time it took her to slink, camouflaged, out of the camp and into a shrouded forest..

Grace Epstein

Grace is a former English and Literature professor from Ohio who followed her family down to Florida two years ago, where she now writes full time. She has published scholarly articles, fiction, and drama and had six plays staged in various parts of the US.

MARK NEWHOUSE'S
TOP TEN PICKS

MABLE'S FIGHT

Mable Oxenfist mopped the last patch of kitchen floor and leaned on the mop handle, crossing her rubber-gloved hands. She inhaled the chemical smell of disinfectant mixed with lemon cleaner and the undertones of vinegar she used on the glass. Can't be too careful nowadays. She adjusted the mask on her face and pinched the nosepiece to make a tighter seal. COVID-19 could kiss her ample behind. No way the blasted Chinese bug was going to get her.

She wiped sweat off her forehead with a Steri-Wipe and looked around.

The kitchen sparkled from ceiling fan to light switches. Not one fingerprint or speck of dirt would dare be found anywhere in her home. She allowed herself a self-satisfied whistle as she plopped the mop in its bucket and rolled it to the proper place in the broom closet. A place for everything and everything in its—what the darn heck?

Three telltale tracks snaked out from behind the bucket, one for each of the wheels. She whirled around and looked closer at her freshly mopped floor. The dirty little trails mocked her as her gaze followed their wiggly progress. She now knew what to look for; she saw more dirty evidence, faint but noticeable, disappear through the doorway. She stepped carefully, avoiding any damp areas, and hurried to the hall. Sure as sugar there they were, marching down the hall and into the kitchen pretty as you please.

"So that's how you want to play it?" She jumped at the sound of her own voice. She hadn't heard a live human in her house in a long while, but it sounded nice for a change, and she continued talking. "I have closets full of rags, and I bought a dozen jugs of industrial cleaner from Costco. Mable Oxenfist doesn't back down from a fight—from man or bug."

The loud bravado thrilled her, and she set her mind for the work ahead. She plucked her tight coveralls away from her body as best she could and fanned herself. Her previous exertions worked up quite a sweat. She felt flushed and a little faint with anticipation.

She grabbed a fresh wad of rags, cracked open a new jug of Clorox Kitchen and Bath and tightened her kneepads. She would meet the deadly enemy face-to-face. Never let it be said that Mable Oxenfist ever shied from a fight.

Mable crouched, and a few spinal pops and knee cracks later, she slowly hit the floor on her hands and knees. Only way to beat this deadly virus is hand-to-hand, just the way she liked it.

"I'm coming for you, virus!"

The wheel tracks stretched out ahead of her, and Mable followed where they led. First she splashed a hefty dollop of cleaner, and then she wiped and wiped until the floor shone like a dinner plate.

Scoot forward and repeat.

Breathing came heavy by then, flooding her cheeks and chin with hot, moist air behind the mask. Only the fear of inhaling a breath of Chinese death kept it in place. Mable viewed it as a trial, a penance, the harsh price she must pay for ultimate victory.

Perspiration poured down her neck and under her arms. She imagined the cuffs of her pants and arm sleeves where she'd taped them tight, soggy and waterlogged with her bodily fluids. At least they were her fluids and not someone else's.

She pressed on until not a single mark from that dingley-darned bucket remained. Mable dropped the last rag from a cramping hand and sat back to catch her breath. Her breathing whooshed in and out like the blacksmith bellows on her dad's old forge.

Wow! Haven't thought of him in ages.

"Don't worry about me, Father. I'm carrying on to the end like you taught me. Job's not done till it's done. Right?"

It occurred to her that the job would not be done until she dealt with the root of the problem, Mr. Mop Bucket, sitting fat and guilty as sin in the broom closet.

Mable crawled over to a kitchen chair. One hand on the seat and then two, she gathered waning reserves of strength and heaved herself up, up to an unsteady vertical. A might creaky, maybe, wobbling like her drunk daddy in a windstorm, but standing, dang it all. Unbeaten and most important, uninfected.

She walked back across tile floor she'd just crawled over, watching critically for any spots she may have missed. Nope. Danged tile was CDC clean. All she had left to do was clean the cause of the mess, that blessed bucket, and she could rest. Finally. Draw a cool breath and shuck this do-it-yourself hazmat fashion statement for a cool shower.

But first . . .

The broom closet still stood open, the red bucket with the spin mop head attachment waiting for her guilty as an egg-sucking dog. She lifted the mop into the spinner and dried it as best she could. She lifted the bucket by the handle.

Now what? The wheels on the bottom were the problem. Probably had dirt packed inside the flimsy plastic wheels. The whole shebang probably made in China. Plastic China wheels. Packed with China virus.

Mable hefted the bucket in two hands, considering her options. Could she spray the wheels off in the sink, or were they too dirty and in need of a good hosing outside? Only way to know was to take a quick peek. Nothing too close. Nothing too long. No sense inviting the virus to jump on her for a ride.

She lifted the bucket as high as her quivering arms could manage. The hands-and-knees scrub session had taken a lot out of her, but she was doing it. The remaining water and cleaner inside the bucket sloshed back and forth and tilted the bucket side to side in her hands.

She shifted her grip to gain a better hold, but her wet hands, tired from their earlier chores, slipped. The bucket tilted toward her. She tried to stop it, but she couldn't. Eyes wide, she watched the gray, soapy, infected water rush toward her face and then gush down her front. Even through her coveralls she felt the water, cool at first and then cold, and then downright freezing.

***

"Get those wet sheets off her; she's freezing. Come on, come on. We've done this twenty times today, people. We are not losing this woman too."

"Fever's a hundred and eight, Doctor."

"Wipe her down. Cool her off. Pour a whole bottle of alcohol on her, if you have to. At least we have enough of that."

The ICU nurses in full PPE—gowns, gloves, masks, and shields—danced around the still form of Mable Oxenfist in a tragically well-practiced choreography.

"Ventilator's doing its job. Now let's do ours."

"Crank the oxygen all the way. I want to hear it. Come on, folks; she's drowning right before our eyes. Move it. I said move it!"

Frances Hight

Frances Hight is an award-winning mystery/thriller writer with ties to critique groups in San Francisco and Orlando. She's a member of MWA and FWA, and a 2018 Royal Palm Literary Award Winner for her unpublished crime novel, Death of a Tomato. Her work has appeared multiple times in FWA Collections.

MARK NEWHOUSE'S TOP TEN PICKS

THE GRAYING

Carla wrapped herself in a warm coat and adjusted her scarf before heading out into the night. She quickened her steps and lowered her head against the chilly wind, pulling the collar of her coat up to cover her face as she did so. The moonless sky made it almost impossible for her to see the path in front of her, but after three months of this, her eyes adjusted quickly to the lack of light and she was able to navigate her way unaided toward the dim lights of the town. She was on a mission, but not sure if this time she would succeed.

She tried to ignore the sounds emanating from the woods on either side of the foot path. The wild animals had become emboldened, their fear of humans greatly diminished since The Event. She reached into her coat pocket and flicked the safety off the Ruger. She hesitated for a moment, trying to determine if she should take it out, but decided to wait. Her senses heightened, she kept her hand on the gun and continued on her way, one foot placed in front of the other, determination driving her forward.

The clouds parted briefly. She could see the main road up ahead bathed in moonlight. It was busy with mainly women, each one walking silently, and separately, braced and ready for battle against the wind, and each other. Carla had journeyed this route before, and had learned firsthand that, indeed, "hell hath no fury like a woman scorned." Figuratively speaking, of course. They were not dealing with rejection, but the stakes were high, and losing was emotionally painful. This time, defeat was not an option for her. This time would be different. She could sense it in her bones, and in her lean, muscled body. The hours she had devoted to training for this very moment would finally pay off.

Leaving the dirt path and stepping onto the asphalt, she relaxed her grip on the gun and dropped her arms to her sides to gain more momentum. Eyes straight ahead, she resisted the urge to glance to the left or right as she power-walked past the shrouded figures who stood between her and her destination. She was thankful for the moonlight while it lasted.

As the clouds closed around her beacon, she slowed her pace. Suddenly, a hand reached out and touched her elbow. She resisted the urge to turn around, and quickened her pace instead. Again, the hand touched her. It was a common delaying tactic. Biting her lip and pulling her collar tighter, she soldiered on.

The flickering lights from the town were barely enough to see the queue, but as she joined the line a commotion erupted up ahead. It was too dark to see what was going on, but she knew. Someone had cut ahead in the line, and a fight had broken out. It was a nightly occurrence, and she still had a bruise above her left eye to remind her that once the line was established, it was best to respect it. Tonight, she would do just that. It was the last time she wanted to travel this route to get what she needed.

The security team of burly men with reflective vests and billy clubs stood on either side of the line, their arms crossed. As Carla got closer to the source of the commotion, she saw two women, their scarves askew, sitting on the ground with their backs to each other, weeping unashamedly. One of the guards approached them, stamped their hands, and sent them on their way. When the ink wore off, they could try again. Carla instinctively glanced at her own hand again to be certain there were no traces of ink left, then shuffled ahead as the line continued to slowly snake its way forward.

Every time she stood in this line, she felt foolish. The women who had already succeeded in making it to the entry point did not have to sneak around under cover of darkness. They were willing and able to avoid the night line reserved for non-essentials only. She hoped after tonight she could get out during the day again so her husband, Jack, did not have to do all the shopping.

A wisp of hair flew into her face. She self-consciously pushed it back and adjusted her scarf, pulling it forward to rest just above her eyebrows. The wind had finally died down, and the tension had begun to ease from her shoulders, and the crowd in general. Their places in line established and secure, they could wait in relative peace and quiet for the doors of the shop to open. Once that happened, there would be electricity in the air, even if there was none in the shop itself.

The line began to move in earnest. She could see the security supervisor with his clicker as he counted out a group of ten, then halted the line to wait. It would be fifteen minutes before the next group would be nodded ahead; just enough time for the first group to exit out the back door. And so it would go, until the clicker read 100, when the rest of the line would be dispersed to try again the next week.

It was hard to tell how many people were ahead of her, but within half an hour she surmised she was in the sixth group, which was especially good since the later groups' luck was hit or miss. Sometimes what they had come for was there; other times the pickings were slim to none.

She had brought her own bag, tucked into her waistband. When she was finally clicked in, she pulled it out, and raced into the shop. Finding exactly what she wanted, and, with tears streaming down her face, she pulled her meager cash savings out of her pants pocket, paid the cashier, and dashed out the back door.

***

She could see smoke curling above the chimney as she approached the small brick house. *Good, they've been doing the prep work I asked them to do, she thought.* Pushing through the front door, she slipped off her coat and scarf, then nodded at Jack as Sophie and JJ threw their arms around her neck. Jack stepped aside, and pointed her toward the bathroom. Clutching her bag, she rushed in, slamming the door behind her.

Trembling, she reached into the bag, opened the box inside, slipped on the cheap plastic gloves, mixed half the chemicals like an old pro, then took one last glance at herself in the mirror. The basin of warm water felt glorious as she plunged her head into it, then applied Clairol 5N Medium Neutral Brown "New Improved" Nice & Easy to three inches of gray roots before easing the dye through her hair to the ends.

When she was done, she stored the unused half of the chemicals in the vent to keep them safe, then applied the lipstick she had also acquired. She was set for another six weeks. The illusion of youth complete, she rejoined her family, looking forward to venturing into town during daylight hours once again.

Janet Palmer

Janet Karr Palmer was born and raised in Western New York and also lived in Massachusetts and Michigan. She is now retired and lives in The Villages, Florida with her husband, Mark. She enjoys writing, editing, reading, bowling, nature, spending time with her family, entertaining, decorating, and walking her two dogs.

MARK NEWHOUSE'S TOP TEN PICKS

THE SAFE TREE

"Thanks love," I say to my wife while leaning back on the sofa cushions. "This is a really good Martini."

I sit in the safety of our home during an imposed confinement against a virus ripping apart the fabric of society, sheltering in place to avoid a silent insidious killer. It's meant to keep us safe, but could that be a mere illusion? It reminds me of a different time of sheltering during World War II. In 2020 our family has security and adequate food, even if we might order it online to be delivered. We have not been issued ration books or had government air-raid shelters built in our back yard.

During the war, rationing in Britain created a carbohydrate rich diet, and those who later calculated sanitation demands estimated that the amount of excrement rose by 250%. Ironically, our biggest problem from the viral attack in 2020 is an illusory shortage of toilet paper.

On a visit to London with my wife a few years ago I felt a need to look for the house of my early memories. Psychologists explain such a desire in many ways. Mine was curiosity. Or so I thought. The search was harder than I expected. Between society's insatiable demands for growth, and the difference in perspective from a that of the five-year-old child, I struggled to imagine Parkside Avenue as it had been. Everything looked much smaller, the road narrower. More houses had been built across the street, filling once open fields. And the houses on our side of the street once destroyed, had been rebuilt.

The street rose to a road running along the crest of a hill, the highest point in the area. I felt compelled to revisit it, to find the spot where I once stood with my mother 70 years before, when we were caught in the open during an air raid in the closing years of WW II.

But let me start at the beginning.

In the summer of 1944, our house, a semi-detached, more familiar as a duplex, was the only one still standing on our side of the street. The houses opposite had been gutted by incendiaries. The road between lay scarred by hardening puddles of melted asphalt, the relics of burned out incendiaries that missed their target.

My mother and I spent part of many nights, between the warning siren and the all-clear, in a darkened room amid the crash and thunder of anti-aircraft guns and bombs. We huddled under a mattress below the dining table, avoiding our government provided shelter in the garden, now a flooded home for rats. Blankets draped over the table prevented stray beams violating the mandatory blackout. It also protected us from the flying glass from broken windows.

She taught me to read by flashlight.

On a late summer morning in 1944, the county bordering the east of London had been eerily quiet. The night before, several of our windows had fallen victim to the blasts of gun and bomb. That morning we found an eight inch piece of jagged shrapnel embedded on the concrete outside the back door. We had heard the shriek of its fall and the thud of its strike. My mother needed to report this bomb damage so we walked to the reporting office, a temporary wooden shed, on the road running along the crest of the hill a quarter mile from our home.

Small weeds and flowers struggled in the rubble beside the road undeterred by the conflict as if they would not be cowed. Maybe they expected that the violence would eventually end. I remember shaking free of her hand to pick a small flower gleaming with yellow petals. I held it up at arms-length below her chin to see the golden reflection on her skin as she sometimes did to me.

We had barely reached the reporting office when the tranquility was interrupted by the rising and falling wail of the air raid siren. Roofers on the school opposite scrambled for the ladders and slid to safety. The tree-lined avenue lay deserted. A gentle breeze. A clear sky. No shelter.

Then the silence was interrupted by the characteristic buzz of a Doodle-Bug, a V1 flying bomb, a vengeance weapon, *Vergeltungswaffe 1*. An early cruise missile. A Nazi terror weapon designed to crash when its fuel ran out. An indiscriminate killer seeking victims of chance. Later I learned the V1 attacks had begun not long before, in June of that year.

Seventy years later, I stood on the avenue with my wife. The school across the road was still there. If it had changed, I couldn't tell. It no longer looked like the enormous building I remembered. The two floors to the roof seemed to have shrunk. But what I had hoped to see had not survived three-quarters of a century. The magnificent Elm trees that once lined the avenue were gone.

"I think it was about here," I told her, waving my hand at the strip of grass between the sidewalk and the roadway where a tree once stood.

"Mum hugged me, I clutched her skirt, and we huddled against the trunk of an Elm. The Doodle-bug flew directly above us, a small silver cross against the blue sky."

Some images you never forget. Like my safe tree.

"It was directly above us when its engine stopped. It blew up several miles away."

Why had I returned? To recapture an emotion that I couldn't identify or to remember my mother's courage? How frightened she must have been, exposed to such danger with her only child.

It wasn't until the war was over that my mother told me that our Doodle-bug had flown over my grandparents' house. Looking over the peaceful country with my wife, I remembered the direction it flew and felt a chill as I realized the significance.

Encouraged by the government to support the nation's self sufficiency, Grandad raised rabbits and chickens in the back garden. I remembered potato peelings, stale bread crusts, and scraps of food saved in a bucket and boiled in a large pot to feed the hens. Their eggs were a precious commodity.

"The rabbits were meant for food but we never ate any."

The war ended with the rabbits blissfully unaware how close they had been to the pot, any more than I understood the threat hanging over us that morning under the tree. My mother had sheltered me as surely as Grandad's hens summoned their chicks and squatted over them in illusory protection against stoats and weasels.

"But how safe did you feel?" my wife asked as we stood on the hilltop

"As safe as my trust in my mother."

What can be more secure than hugging a mother's skirt, with her arm around you? Or huddling under a mattress? Maybe I was only as secure as the chicks, but I know that at the time the illusion of security was complete.

Could we tolerate life without the security of illusion? Could we survive in a world of reality? Could we trust our memories?

I find I am fiercely clutching the cushion fabric. My fingers tremble as I reach for another Martini.

Robert Hart

A retired veterinarian, Bob and his novelist wife, Veronica Helen, live in Ormond Beach. Author of several articles and stories, three pet books, and a book of short stories, he is a frequent contributor to the annual FWA Collections.

MARK NEWHOUSE'S
TOP TEN PICKS

CANCELED

Jake shook his head the sheet of paper lying surrounded by dust on his old rolltop. He could deal with sloppy housekeeping. It was the credit card statement that made him scowl. According to American Express, his bill had been paid in full including his new Bose sound system, his card canceled, and the account closed. He'd been an AmEx member for years. How could they do this to him?

Margaret.

He wouldn't put it past his wife to devise a spiteful stunt like this. Not that he'd confront her with his suspicion. She could slice him like a French baguette then accuse him of making crumbs. If only she would go away and leave him in peace. Margaret did just that, moving out of their one-bedroom apartment first. The plan, that he would stay until the place sold, gave him the calm and quiet he craved. But did he trust she wouldn't come back?

There had to be a story here—guy in the throes of bitter divorce lives quiet life on edge without credit. Waiting for apartment to sell, guy succumbs to accumulated dust. He'd sold a few personal essays to the New Yorker. Would they buy this one? Margaret verbally shredded his last attempt, "Living on the Fringe—A Man's Perspective of Mascara."

"What do you know about waterproof formulas, eye makeup remover, and lash curlers heated or otherwise? No one will buy it. It's garbage."

That was months ago. He hadn't had a creative idea since. Expecting the dam of writer's block to burst once Margaret left, nary a trickle seeped out. His energy level, normally low and a favorite hot spot for Margaret's carping, had slowed to inertia; the swiping of dust a Herculean effort. Time hung on him like an old baggy sweater he was loath to shrug off.

Jake stepped into the living room from the cramped alcove housing his desk. Aiming a kick at a small stack of packing cartons, he missed. He could hear Margaret now, berating him for being "aimless." Connecting wouldn't have mattered though. The boxes contained the dregs of their possessions; items Margaret deemed unworthy of taking with her. Each carton of assorted leftovers wore a label of contents in a precise, feminine hand. Like his marriage, an orderly union of things disconnected, completely orchestrated by his soon-to-be-ex wife.

A key in the door broke the silence. Jake froze.

Margaret?

His breathing eased as a frizzy-haired realtor shouldered her way in. A pair of prospective buyers followed. Though annoyed he hadn't been informed of the showing, he kept the complaint to himself. Margaret's gnawing at his lack of backbone aside, he didn't want negative vibes clouding a potential sale. Jake waved, sidling back into the alcove and calling out, "Hi, folks. Don't mind me. Just pretend I'm not here."

The ill-mannered couple did just that, ignoring him without a greeting in return. The realtor waved, but only as a sweep of her arm to encompass the room.

"You can see the apartment gets good light. Let me show you the rest of the place."

Jake settled in his cracked leather chair at the hand-me-down desk; what he referred to as antiques to Margaret's label of junk. Sounds of the tour carried to his niche: kitchen cabinet doors banging closed, the toilet flushing, chatter about the view. He didn't want to interrupt but if they wanted the real view, they were too early for the show.

Every evening, perfectly framed by the bathroom window, the Empire State Building lit up like a gothic neon-scape. The scene so captivated Jake, he'd taken to bathing in the tub at night with the lights out. Contrary to Margaret's snide remarks about missed body parts rotting from going unwashed, he didn't need illumination to soap up.

The more his wife harped on his lavatory escapes, the more Jake took shelter there. It incensed her that he hogged the room, though he left the door unlocked for her to enter as she pleased. She fumed over wet towels puddled on the floor—cold, squishy, mounds that lay in wait for the unwary when nature called in the middle of the night. If Margaret's surprised screech woke Jake, he had no trouble falling back to sleep.

Oblivious to Margaret's precise decorating style—miniature glass dachshunds arranged in a litter of vignettes; antique paper fans splayed at exacting angles—Jake added to his sanctuary. He purchased a Bose sound system, installing it on a make-shift shelf above the bathroom's crystal-finial towel bars. Margaret's repertoire of anatomically impossible curses rolled out like toilet paper. Two days later she had everything packed and labeled. By the time the movers came, Jake was into long soaks and loud Debussy. If his wife snarked a parting comment, he didn't know. He never heard her leave.

Would the young couple now exploring the apartment appreciate that majestic view? Probably not the wife—she wore the pinched-lips of swallowed vinegar. He felt sorry for the husband. If these two bought the place, he'd suggest the guy purchase a Bose.

The realtor paced at the front door while the couple took a second look around. About to call out and mention the bathroom view after dark, Jake paused at the pair's hasty return.

"What do you think? Could you see yourselves living here after what happened?"

Though dwarfed by her bullmastiff of a mate, the petite young woman took charge. Jake cringed in sympathy when, with a flick of her finger, she stopped her husband from speaking.

"I don't know. The bathroom looks so clean. Everything's scrubbed and painted. It's hard to imagine."

The husband ducked his head in submission. "But don't you think the layout would work for us, honey?"

Jake listened to their exchange. Even with reservations they sounded interested. A sale could mean the end of Margaret's harassment; the impetus for him to move on. He came out of the alcove and ambled over to the group, clearing his throat and putting on a friendly smile. But irritation linked his brows when again he was ignored.

The young woman continued to dominate the conversation. "It would be perfect … except … I don't think we'd have a moment's peace here." She leaned into the realtor with a shiver. "I heard the husband got electrocuted while taking a bath. They say his wife tossed some piece of audio equipment into the tub as she was moving out."

The husband inched closer to his wife. "And they say the guy never saw it coming 'cause music was blasting and the lights were off."

Margaret!

Jake's hands fisted in anger—like his credit card account, he'd been canceled too. Then a deep sigh of relief softened his hold— Margaret would bother him no more. Turning from the group, he stepped down the hall to the bathroom and settled himself in the tub. It was almost showtime.

Though the man did not return, intuition led Manny to continue remitting the man's fifteen percent fee. After all, he thought, a writer is entitled to his royalties.

And he was no longer hurting.

Barbara Rein

Barbara writes her nightmares, having grown up on macabre fairy tales and endless episodes of Twilight Zone. She lives with her husband and dachshund, splitting time and writing groups between New York and Florida.

MARK NEWHOUSE'S TOP TEN PICKS

YELLOW LEAF IN A PUDDLE

She slid into the booth at the Cheesecake Factory in Sarasota, her usual vision of vibrancy. From her crystal studded sandals to the frosted tips of her tousled hair she glowed with good health and exuberant energy. Her blue eyes scanned the menu then she set it aside so we could immediately begin catching up on each other's news.

My sister was a "snowbird" who wintered in Florida every year from January through May. It was only March but already she had a deep golden tan. A veteran journalist and avid world traveller, she was able to transfer her skills and experience into a productive second career which allowed her to work, via computer, anywhere in the world. She told me the business was doing well and she absolutely loved her work. She was joyfully living her dream life.

Even with my nurse-trained eyes, I saw no hint that I would soon look back on this "picture of perfect health" as an illusion. But six weeks after she had returned to Canada, I received the word.

"Today did not go as planned. I'm taking a new life journey."

My dear younger sister was diagnosed with a large malignant tumor in her kidney as well as an extremely aggressive pancreatic cancer already involving lymph nodes. She would need extensive surgery followed by months of chemotherapy.

I flew home to be at her side. Though she appeared physically weak, and had turned mustard yellow from jaundice, her humor and jovial personality had not changed. She was accepting the known and the unknown with equanimity. She would talk about her cancer for a while and then say, "now let's talk about other things."

And we did. We covered many topics and had many laughs despite the gravity of her prognosis. I could only stay two weeks on that visit but I promised to return for her birthday in September, secretly praying she would still be there.

When I returned in the fall she was thinner and weaker but still managed her big smiles. She had her nails manicured in vivid rose and wore lipstick to match. With her hair gone from the chemo treatments, she wore glamorous head scarves always coordinated with her stylish, colorful tops. We still had our laughs, but we had serious talks as well. When I asked how she was really doing, this highly accomplished, well-educated woman looked intently at me and honestly replied.

"Nothing I have trained for, nothing I have been through, has prepared me for this experience."

She was on a new journey. Unlike her many trips all over the world, this was an uncharted excursion, with uncertain timelines and an unknown outcome. She didn't know what currency to use in this foreign country of cancer, except courage, determination and acceptance.

She only knew "today." Everything but the current moment was slipping through her fingers. She closed her business, took care of her personal affairs, and even planned her funeral to every little detail. Then she went on living to the extent that she was able.

One day she said, "Sis, since I've been diagnosed, it's like I have this heightened awareness of life. I'm noticing so many things I used to miss."

"Be careful," I teased her, "you might end up writing poetry."

A few weeks later she admitted that she was actually hand-writing in a journal. This mile-a-minute typist discovered that slow writing helped her get in touch with her deeper emotions more easily than pounding a computer keyboard. Accustomed to a broad and thoroughly organized life with schedules laid out months in advance, she was now trying to adjust to "the unplanned life" as she called it. The wide circumference of her pre-diagnosis life shrunk to a narrow circle. Her weakened immune system and risk of infection caused her to eliminate contact with all but a few close family members. In confinement, the chrysanthemums blooming on her doorstep or a pool of sunlight on her wood floor took on greater significance.

The surgery was brutal. The chemo was devastating, but it bought her a few months, allowing one last Christmas with her family. On February 25 I flew home to Canada again, arriving just in time to hold my sister's hand one last hour before she slipped away.

On the day of her funeral, March first, Florida's first case of Covid-19 was diagnosed. In one week my perspective on the world, both personally and globally, had changed forever. I was forced to confront the illusions I had created.

I had lost an older brother to cancer years ago. It was difficult, but there was some layer of expectation that older siblings would predecease younger ones. I had created an illusion that my younger sister would outlive me. I had created an illusion that healthy-looking people would not suddenly get sick and die.

I knew I would return saddened after the funeral, but I had created the illusion that I would return to a stable world, giving me time to slowly grieve and recover peacefully. Nothing I had ever experienced prepared me for learning that a "cancer," and a highly contagious one at that, would infect the entire globe. I had created an illusion that something like this would never happen, or at the very least, if it did, we would have warning and be given lead time to prepare for its impact. We would all be told to go get a haircut, stock up on supplies, visit our loved ones and hug them.

I had created an illusion of peace and security, even in a large, heavily populated state like Florida. As the lockdown orders expanded and unemployment increased drastically, a sense of restlessness became apparent. A murder occurred in our small town; a week later, a second one added to the tension.

I longingly recalled the peaceful drive I had taken through the gentle landscape of rural Nova Scotia en route to the Halifax Airport for my flight home after my sister's death.

My thoughts turned to "moving back."

"I want to go home and live in a smaller, safer region," I told my husband.

The next night the news blared. A massive shooting had just taken place with an unknown number of victims in rural Nova Scotia. A crazed man on a murderous mission left a trail of bloodshed over a forty mile swath. The horror of twenty-two violent fatalities, and several injured survivors, inflicted an area already suffering from the impact of the coronavirus pandemic.

Another illusion I had created had crumpled. Safer elsewhere? Safety nowhere.

What I am left to confront is my willingness and ability to look at life with brutal honesty and accept its vicissitudes with the grace with which my sister accepted her cancer. It has brought me also to a "heightened awareness" of life. This morning I saw a yellow oak leaf trembling in a bronze puddle. It was as if everything I had seen before was but a gray blur and suddenly I witnessed brilliant yellow for the first time. Small beauty, fragile joy, I'll take it.

Phyllis McKinley

Phyllis McKinley brought her passion for writing with her when she moved to Florida from the Canadian Maritimes. Recipient of multiple RPLA awards, and author of five books, Phyllis loves books, nature, and people, not necessarily in that order. Her stories appear in six previous FWA Collections.

MASKS OF CLAY

I rubbed my face. Its cold porcelain smoothness comforted me.

"Don't touch it, Maeve."

Mother was not here to scold me, but her shrill correction, often repeated, echoed in my head.

I lowered my hand.

School dismissed ten minutes ago. Since Mother had not come to meet me, I would walk home alone. My classmates gathered in their usual way, clusters that did not include me.

"Maeve! Want to walk home with us?"

I touched my face again to check that the porcelain mask had not shifted. Then I turned to find the girl who called my name. Bridget waved at me from across the parking apron. Neither she nor her friends wore masks. They had not scratched away their beauty.

I waited for Bridget's "just kidding." Her friends held hints of sneers in the corners of their lips. They waited for her "just kidding," too.

I was glad they could not see my expression.

"Well?" Bridget beckoned again. "Aren't you coming?"

I devised reasons for Bridget's unexpected generosity. Maybe she felt sorry for me. Maybe she wanted to appear charitable in front of the teachers. A tiny sliver of hope penetrated my heart. Maybe today I would join the "in" crowd.

The girls began to walk away, but Bridget waited for me. Still wary, I shuffled forward. She grabbed my hand. "Let's go."

The afternoon sun did nothing to cut the late fall chill, and we dodged frigid shadows etched in the sidewalk by the ancient oaks lining our town's Main Street. I listened to the idle chatter of the girls around me. They recited a litany of gossip: unfair teachers, oblivious boys, and annoying girls. They had nothing nice to say, so I said nothing.

One girl broke free of the herd and turned up the driveway of a modest brick house. A sudden chorus erupted around me.

"Bye, Nancy!"

"See you in the morning."

Their warmth and sincerity charmed me. What must it be like to walk home with friends every day? Mother walked with me most days. She needed the exercise, she told me, because Father would not love her if she grew fat and ugly. I wondered if he loved me now that I was scared and ugly. Hard to tell. Father wore a different kind of mask.

Other people wore porcelain masks like mine. The Pox afflicted everyone, some worse than others. I caught it three years ago. Mother blamed me for my disfiguration. "I told you not to scratch them," she'd scold me in the same scathing tone each morning while threading the mask's laces through my thick brown hair. "You couldn't stop touching them."

She was right, of course. The round, itchy sores had driven me to distraction. I picked and picked at them until I dug craters into my skin. Now I had to wear a mask. No one wanted to see my hideous face.

Bridget squeezed my hand and gave me a tiny smile. "How was your day?"

"Okay, I guess." I'd never seen her this close before. Her flawless skin glowed in the afternoon sun.

"Oh wow. Look at her. She's got more craters than the moon."

My head snapped up. The insult came from a girl in our group, but it wasn't directed at me. A maskless woman—a Pox victim—walked towards us with two bags of groceries in her arms. Her raw skin curled around dozens of oozing, crusty sores.

Whispers and snickers proliferated around me.

"Yuck. If I looked like that, I wouldn't go out in public."

"Maybe she just needs to wash her face."

"Hey, pizza face," a bold girl shouted, "cover it up!"

The woman reached us. She paused in our midst, clutching her groceries like a shield. "You girls should be ashamed of yourselves." The scabs on her furrowed brow puckered. "My condition doesn't embarrass me."

The bold girl snorted. "It should. Your nasty face is ruining my day."

The woman's gaze settled on me. "A Pox victim's ugliness can be concealed." She gave me a wink and smiled at the smirking girl. "Too bad yours can't." Chin held high, she pushed past us.

The girls stood in shocked silence until one of them muttered, "I bet her husband left her."

"Yeah. Her kids probably cry every time they look at her."

Bridget tugged my arm. "Let's get out of here." She guided me down a side street, away from her friends. "Is it that bad? Your face, I mean?"

I stiffened. Now I understood Bridget's interest in me. She wanted to see the freak behind the mask. I yanked my hand free. "Wasn't that woman entertainment enough for you?"

"Wait! Maeve..."

My feet pounded against uneven pavement. The alley merged with another and opened into a small courtyard. The courtyard's only tenant, an ice cream shop, was closed.

Dead leaves rustled beneath my feet. I slowed to a stop in front of a bubbling fountain and stared down at the water's rippling surface. My reflection danced, a thousand broken shards.

A minute later, Bridget's distorted face appeared next to mine. "Don't be mad. I didn't mean to upset you."

I sat on the fountain's stone rim, and she sat beside me. Misery squeezed my heart. I wanted to believe her. My fingers stirred the cool, sparkling water. Copper coins, forgotten wishes, littered the fountain's tiled basin. "Another girl asked to see my face, once." I hesitated. Three years later, the memory still stung. "I thought she was being friendly."

"I never asked to see your face." Bridget dipped her hand in the fountain. A palmful of water splashed against her cheek, and creamy clay dribbled down her chin. "I was trying to tell you something." More handfuls of water washed away carefully blended powder and clay. "I'll show you instead."

Silt dyed the fountain's clear water beige. I stared at Bridget' pock-marked face. She looked no different than me.

"I had no idea," I said.

Pox-concealing cosmetics were not expensive, but Mother refused to purchase them for me. I did this to myself, she told me, and I would suffer the consequences, a porcelain mask the penance for my disobedience.

Bridget touched her bare skin. "I have to be so careful. If I smile, the clay might crack. If I cry, it runs. I don't want anyone to know how ugly I am."

"You aren't ugly."

Her scarred skin split to reveal a brilliant smile. "Neither are you."

I wanted her to see the smile hidden beneath my mask. "Help me untie these laces."

Ruth Alessi

After a couple decades of toying with other mediums, Ruth has settled upon writing as a way to share the ideas in her head. Like all artists, she hopes others will enjoy her creations, but mostly she is happy to find she is not alone.

Alternate Universes

"Don't try to explain the formula. Just show that the mathematics work. Most people don't understand gravity, let alone alternate universes," Zolton said as Ellen finished her manuscript.

Ellen did as Zolton suggested. He was the guiding voice in her head that had been there since she could remember. Her parents were convinced that once Ellen started school and made other friends, the imaginary Zolton would disappear, but he didn't.

"It is best not to mention me to others," Zolton told Ellen when she started kindergarten. "Hearing a voice in your head is considered a sign of illness, and you are not ill. Talking to me is like talking to God. People don't see God, but they talk to him all the time."

"Are you God?" Ellen asked.

"No, like you, I am a creation of God—just a more spiritual one."

Zolton never gave orders, just suggestions, and Ellen usually did what Zolton suggested. A few times she defied him, such as when she and two friends got very ill drinking vodka, or when she got into an accident after her father said the roads were too icy to drive.

In the summer before her senior year in high school, Ellen fell in love with Carl, former cap-tain of the football team, who was going away to college that fall. "He's like my hero Lochinvar, in the poem by Sir Walter Scott," she told Zolton. "A strong warrior who would ride across the moors of Scotland to save me from a life without love."

"Love takes many forms, and romantic love like you feel for Carl doesn't always last. It was devised to keep your species going, but it often leads to pain and disappointment," Zolton warned. "It would be best if you ended it now."

Ellen didn't end it. "You are wrong about Carl," Ellen said. "Carl and I will marry, have children, and live happily ever after."

"You were meant for more important things," Zolton said, but to Ellen that summer, nothing was more important than Carl. She saw him every day and heard Zolton's voice less and less. Af-ter Carl went off to college, she wrote him sometimes twice a day, though she heard from him far less. In late October Carl asked Ellen to come to the college for homecoming, but her father wouldn't let her go. She decided to surprise Carl by going anyway. She told her parents that she was staying overnight at a girlfriend's house, and she and the girlfriend drove to the college. To her surprise Zolton didn't object. When she got to Carl's room there was a Do Not Disturb sign on the door. She knocked anyway.

"Didn't you see the sign?" the young man who opened the door said.

Ellen asked for Carl.

"It was Carl's turn to have the room last night with his date, so now it's my turn. Who are you anyway?"

Ellen was devastated, and she and her friend drove back home.

"I tried to warn you," Zolton said. "He didn't deserve your love."

Ellen was not the same after that. She was quieter, more reserved, and less trusting. She con-centrated on her studies and became more dependent on Zolton. She had perfect scores on her SATs, went to school at the California Institute of Technology, and finished all her studies in record time. She had her choice of graduate schools and settled on MIT. Ellen told her advisor that she wanted to explore the theoretical aspects of alternate universes and find a way to defy distance and time. Her social life for the next two years consisted of joining a running club and occasionally having dinner with members of her lab. Her main focus was her research, and her main friend was Zolton.

"We did it," Zolton said as Ellen finished her thesis. "It makes me sad that our work is done."

"Why would you be sad?" Ellen asked. She poured herself a glass of wine.

Zolton didn't answer right away. "This work will open up a new field of physics and ensure your place in science. You will be another Einstein or Newton."

"I couldn't have done it without you, and I am no Einstein," Ellen said. "Maybe I should have acknowledged you in my thesis. I'm not sure it's fair for me to take all the credit."

"That would greatly confuse things," Zolton said. "A voice in your head is no more believa-ble than a Lochinvar riding across the moors of Scotland."

Ellen raised her glass. "Zolton, you are my Lochinvar. Wouldn't you ride across the moors of Scotland to save me?"

"Yes, I would, Ellen. I would."

***

"Well done, Zolton" Vargas said. "You have given mankind the beginning of the knowledge to reach our galaxy one day. She was the first female whose mind you shared. How did she compare to the others, Aristotle, Newton, or Einstein?"

"It felt different with her."

"The men always did well after you left them. Will she do as well?"

"I expect that she will marry several times, never really finding her Lochinvar, and she will do solid work, but never the level of our discovery. Probably there will be children, so her life will be full, more like Einstein who had several wives and children. Newton didn't like people, and Aristotle never had time for love. Eventually she will conclude that the voice in her head was re-ally her own, just an illusion left over from childhood."

"We may have to use your talents again," Vargas said.

"I'm not sure I would be the best choice." Zolton bowed. "There are younger ones who have fresher minds."

"We will go with your judgment," Vargas said.

Zolton backed out of the room. Once outside, he let his mind wander. He imagined walking toward Ellen in Netherby Hall, as the words of the poem came back. "One touch to her hand, and one word in her ear, / When they reach'd the hall-door, and the charger stood near; / So light to the croupe the fair lady he swung, / So light to the saddle before her he sprung!"

Zolton couldn't tell Vargas the whole truth for fear that Vargas would consider him unsound, but even leaders of advanced civilizations don't know everything. In Vargas' world there was no such thing as love, but after sharing Ellen's thoughts all those years, Zolton missed her and want-ed to part of her life again, even if it meant pain and disappointment. He and Ellen were worlds and times apart, but Zolton felt they were destined to meet again. He believed now that souls could transcend time, distance, and alternate worlds. He would wait for the time when he could ride across the moors of Scotland and save his Ellen.

Monika Becker

A former college professor, Monika Becker has authored many research articles, but her passion was always writing fiction. Since retiring she has published in seven FWA Collections, placed in writing competitions, and made the RPLA finals list numerous times. She resides with her husband in Venice, Florida.

THE TREASURE HUNT

"May we go to the pasture?" I asked in an excited tone hoping Mother would say yes.

"Are the cattle out?"

"No", I answered in a half-truth. I did look but didn't see any… so they're not there.

"All right but be home by five. Do you have your watch?"

"Yes." I answered and rushed to the door. My sister poked along. She has no sense of adventure and didn't want to come, but I bribed her. I promised I'd do the dishes by myself tonight if she'd go. Mother never lets us go anywhere by ourselves. With over-protective parents, my sister and I create our own adventure.

This was going to be my chance to check out the underground spring with the satin smooth pebbles. Some of those stones glisten and sparkle like diamonds, and I'm sure I caught a glimpse of gold shimmering among the little rocks.

I climbed over the four-rung gate and was on the other side. My sister hadn't raised a foot yet. I wanted to run off and leave her, but I knew she'd go back to the house and tell Mother she wasn't going. That would ruin any hopes of finding a sparkling diamond or a little gold nugget.

Brenda is finally over the gate and purposely walks slow to make me mad, but I don't care now. I run ahead towards the sloping hill. Our friend's grandmother owns this land and told us there were treasures buried out in the pasture. And why wouldn't I believe that? Brenda doesn't.

The last time we were here, I drank the water as it bubbled out of the ground. It's cool and clear. My sister said I was drinking cow pee, but I know better. Besides that, she never wants to get her hands dirty and she won't drink the water.

My heart is pounding as I reach the stream. I like to watch the water ooze out and trickle down a pebble-lined path. The ground reclaims the water before it gets very far. I even think the moss-covered rocks are pretty. Brenda thinks they're dirty. I kneeled and scoop up a handful of pebbles and watch the tiny collection slip through my fingers almost like sand. By this time, my sister is by my side. I reached out a handful so she could see the different colors and hopefully she'd sort through the stones. Two sets of eyes are better than one when you're looking for something as important as gold. She stares out towards the barn located on the other end of the pasture.

"You know the cows are in here, don't you?" She exclaimed in a tone crossed between anger and fear. "You lied to Mother!"

"I did not… I said I checked. I did not see a cow when I looked. Besides, they aren't going to hurt us." Sometimes my sister makes me so mad. She doesn't want to do anything but play with the cat. "I will watch just to make sure they don't come this way. Anyway, we can run faster than a cow." That's probably the first thing Brenda will tell Mother when we get home.

I reached down to get another handful of pebbles. My fingers went into a hole. I stuck my hand in further and the hole got bigger, and bigger and then much bigger. "I think I found the treasure," I screamed. "Look Brenda," I yelled as I put my arm in up to my elbow. "I feel something… I really do." I lay on my belly and tried to get a grip on whatever I was feeling. In my mind, it was the treasure chest.

"I'm leaving! The cows are coming and I'm not staying." Brenda turned and run back towards the gate.

I stretched and strained trying to determine if the thing I was touching was a chest. I raised up to see how close the cows were and if Brenda had made it back to the gate hoping she wouldn't go home. She hates doing dishes… maybe she'll wait at the gate.

The hole seems to be getting bigger. It's the size of a burn barrel. I leaned over the edge of the rim peering into total darkness. The water was still oozing to the surface. It was too tempting not to reach into the hole and attempt to pull our whatever was within arm's reach. As I lay down to position myself, the ground gave way and the edge of the hole was under my stomach. It felt like mush underneath me. Just as I was deciding whether to pursue this, a decision wasn't necessary. The hole swallowed me! I grabbed for the edge, but it crumbled in my hand. I yelled at Brenda. She couldn't hear me, because now I was under the ground's surface. Feeling the mud against my legs and arms, I knew I was in trouble. My mother will be upset that I ruined a good set of play clothes.

It was dark in the hole. I couldn't feel anything like a treasure chest. Everything seemed soft and wet, very wet. I tried to grasp something that would allow me to climb out. Everything was soft and mushy. There was a tiny shaft of light and I could make out a wad of fine roots, but that was all. My heart began to pound. I looked up and there stood a cow peering down at me, but not for long. With a squashing sound and a huge glob of mud, the cow was at my side flailing around trying to get her footing. There was no time to think after that. The bottom of the hole opened wider. The cow and I went traveling in what seemed to be a dark tunnel. The cow's hoofs hit me in the face. I tried to hang on to her tail because she ended up in front of me. I couldn't breathe… I was so scared. My arms and legs were going in all direction and not hitting anything. There was water, but not like you'd swim in. It was just splashing against me and the cow. She was still ahead of me because I could feel her tail wrack up against my face. It seemed we were moving in a downward direction. I don't remember thinking I was going to die… I was just scared and wished I hadn't wanted to go treasure hunting. I do remember thinking Brenda would have to do the dishes by herself.

"Would you wake up? You're crowding me out of bed." My sister elbowed me. I sit up and chocked from fear. Later that morning, Brenda asked if I wanted to go for a walk. I told her no, I'd rather stay here and play with the cat.

Linda B. Callan

Linda started writing as a hobby after she retired. Being a member of the Arcadia Writers Group and a member of FWA has kept her motivated to stay on this adventurous journey.

BOOKEND FRIENDS

Valentine's Day wasn't always about candy and flowers. My mom surprised me with a unique Valentine's gift more than fifty years ago. Her thoughtfulness provides a display of love on my nightstand today.

I tore open the heavy box and found a pair of matching heart-shaped brass objects. "What are they?"

"Follow me, and I'll show you," Mom said. She stood the two hearts on their flat ends on my bedroom dresser. "Hand me a few of your scattered books. See? They're bookends. They hold books upright."

That night while lying in bed I noticed something. The bookends glistened in the moonlight. They reminded me of my two close friends, Susan and Diane, who were loyal, supportive, and encouraging when I struggled with a problem. A few months earlier I had auditioned for the high school musical. Several others tried out for the part of lead singer, but the director chose me. Rehearsals went great, but on opening night, someone broke into the band room and vandalized it. Susan and Diane found me in the girl's bathroom wiping my tears with strips of fabric the vandal had ripped from my costume. Susan grabbed some tissues and handed them to me. "I'm so sorry this happened. Do you have a clue who did it?"

"Probably some jealous girls," Diane said, pushing my bangs back.

"How can I sing on stage now? I have nothing to wear."

"Do you want me to look for the choir teacher?" Susan asked. "Maybe she can help."

"I have a better idea," Diane said. "Take off your sequined skirt, Susan."

Susan's jaw dropped. "Do what?"

"Silly girl, you have leggings on. They count as pants." Diane unbuttoned her own blouse to reveal a silky tank top. She tugged her tank top over her head and handed it to me, along with Susan's skirt. "Here's your new costume. Now get going."

At that moment Susan and Diane became genuine friends who opened my mind to new possibilities.

The next day during lunch period, Valentine's Day popped up in the conversation. Diane asked, "Did you get something special?"

"Mom gave me a set of heart-shaped bookends."

Susan elbowed Diane. "Bookends! Who uses bookends anymore? My mom gave me a cute purse with a twenty-dollar bill inside."

I tossed my napkin toward them. "Hey, those bookends remind me of you two."

"How's that?" Susan asked.

"Above all, you both hold a special place in my heart. You're my biggest supporters and always have my back. I think I'll call us bookend friends. What do you think?"

"Sounds like fun. We can start a Bookend Friends Club," Diane said.

Susan winked. "Count me in."

Over the years our friendships deepened. We leaned on each other for inspiration to accomplish our dreams. We made a pact to bear one another's failures and rejoice with each other's victories.

Susan and I planned a surprise graduation party for Diane when she received her degree. I called Diane early one afternoon. "Do you want to grab a quick bite at our favorite restaurant and then catch a movie?"

"Sure. Let's invite Susan to join us."

"I already did. She's not feeling well."

"Ahh, poor thing."

Diane's eyes widened when we walked into the back room of the restaurant decorated with her school colors and balloons. Susan along with a few other friends yelled, "Surprise!" Laughter filled the air while each person brought a humorous story about Diane to the table.

We vowed to visit each other before we moved away. Despite the distance when one of us came down with an illness, we sent cards to brighten the day or called with a message of hope. Often we needed only a few kind words to remind us we're not alone. Their ties grew to be an essential part of my life.

I will never forget how those precious friends held me close during my troublesome divorce. Even though those weeks were a blur to me, I thanked God for my compassionate friends. Diane offered a room in her home. Her concern and guidance kept me safe. Often she sat quietly with me over a cup of tea. Each nod confirmed she understood. Susan faithfully prayed, helping me walk the journey of tears. Through those two friends I learned to trust again.

Later, trying to survive as a single parent, I joined a community of single mothers. During our meetings others often borrowed diapers from me. No one returned the favor. I offered to babysit so they could have a night out. They took advantage and didn't pick up their child when they said they would. I even lent them money when they came up short on their rent. I foolishly thought we would share our struggles in those relationships, but the others never offered me a hand in friendship. They called only if they needed something. It didn't take me long to realize those connections were illusions. They contributed nothing in the way of friendship. It was painful when I realized those acquaintances existed based on rewards.

My bookend friends, however, asked for nothing and gave everything. They nurtured my spirit over the years.

I've learned a lifelong lesson: bundle yourself with bookend friends. Having someone stick beside you and support you for the long haul delivers the perfect ending.

Linda Ray Center

Linda retired from a thirty-two-year career in dance education. She is a hands-on grandmother and will display her grandchildren's pictures at any given moment. As a communicator she encourages women and children to walk in God's love and direction, strengthening one another.

Illusion Tubes

The hallway was sterile and silent. Four first-contact experts sat on two benches looking at four evenly spaced doors on the other side of the hall. Each wore a pressurized suit with their names stitched across their chest. They sat with their helmets in their laps.

Crowe and Kendall sat together with perfect posture, waiting with a masonic blankness for the doors to open. Mayes glanced nervously at them out of the corner of her eye. Next to her, Dodd sighed.

"It all goes back to firing squads," Dodd said.

"What?" Mayes asked. Dodd liked to talk when he was nervous.

"The reason there are four of us," Dodd said, "It all goes back to firing squads. Back in the day, when executing someone, they would give most of the firing squad rifles loaded with blanks, and a few of them rifles loaded with real bullets. That way, the executioners did not have to feel responsible for killing someone. Each person who pulled the trigger knew they probably had a blank."

"We are not killing anyone," Mayes said.

"Hopefully," Dodd replied, "Human history is filled with first contacts that went really badly. Plagues were spread. Cultures were destroyed by colonization. Right now, the United Nations wants to be friends with the universe. Who knows where we will be politically in ten years? Whatever happens, we each get to know it is probably not our fault."

"I have a strong feeling that I am going down there," Mayes said, "I don't think I will be sent to an illusion tube. I think I am really going down there."

"We all feel that," Dodd said, "One of us is right."

Without warning, all four doors opened simultaneously. Each revealed an identical closet-sized room with lighted walls. The four explorers stood and donned their helmets. Each turned to their partner and checked their equipment. Dodd shot Mayes a wink before walking through his door.

Mayes's door closed behind her with a shish followed by a dull thud. The room would transport her either onto the planet below or into an illusion tube where she would experience a simulation so compelling that she would be unable to ascertain if everything around her was real.

She told herself that Dodd was winding her up. He often dealt with stress by trying to make her stressed. Testing showed that people perform better in low-stress situations, thus the illusion tubes. Each explorer could rest easy, knowing that this was probably another practice run.

Mayes suddenly felt like she was on fire. Being transported remained exactly as painful the thousandth time as it was the first. Her body was ripped apart. Each cell cried out in its own isolated panic. She passed out.

When she opened her eyes, the sky above her was obscured by a thin mist dancing on a swirling breeze. She was on her back. Her ship hung above her in low orbit, visible only as a small tube too far away to be seen clearly. Moisture started to collect on her helmet.

Slowly, hesitantly, with an inconsistency that suggested intelligence, something started to obscure her view of the sky. A face unlike any she had ever seen eclipsed her ship. A single eye looked down at her. Mayes blinked, causing the creature to retreat quickly.

Mayes sat up slowly. Every move was a risk. In training, they stressed the necessity of taking calculated risks.

If you encounter a bear in the woods, you make yourself as large as possible and yell so that it will deem you more trouble than you are worth. If you meet a gorilla in the jungle, don't challenge it under any circumstances because it will fight you, and it will win. If you encounter a person, you wave and judge their reaction. Mayes turned towards the alien as she stood, looking for any clues its anatomy provided about its psychology.

They stood considering each other for a moment. Drone reconnaissance of the planet had failed to find anything like this creature. It seemed to breathe through its skin. Thousands of pours perforating its rocky exoderms brought the moisture in the air in and then exhaled it. The mist seemed to bounce around it, vibrating in a consistent rhythm.

The structure of the alien's body was roughly humanoid. Its skin, perhaps an exoskeleton or bone, grew into small formations all over its body that reminded Mayes of coral reefs. These formations increased the alien's surface area as it backed slowly away from her. Mayes decided that the creature was feeding on the moisture by filtering out organic matter. It was neither like a bear nor like a gorilla. Did it have a temperament like a whale? Could it be intelligent?

Mayes raised a hand and slowly waved. The creature waved back.

The wind picked up, lifting the mist. Mayes could see for miles now. The landscape rolled out before her in sharp but beautiful rocky texture. Stone twisted around itself, suggesting violent tectonic upheavals that predated life on Earth. It was breathtaking.

Suddenly Mayes was on fire again. Her body tore apart. She woke up on her back, looking at an off-white ceiling.

A violent, angry depression overtook her as soon as she regained consciousness. It was going so well, why would they call her back? She sat up slowly. Crowe and Kendall were sitting up beside her. Dodd was nowhere to be seen. Four chairs sat facing a glass wall. A man in an expensive suit smiled at them from behind the glass. The three explorers found their chairs.

"Congratulations," The man said, "All three of you did wonderfully. This was one of the best first contacts we have ever had. In a moment, the door behind you will open, and you can all go to your decontamination rooms."

"Where is Dodd?" Mayes asked.

"Unfortunately," the man said, "Dodd made some errors. Fortunately, he was in an illusion tube, so those errors will not affect anything but his career. He will be boarding a shuttle to Earth soon. Because of the shuttle's schedule, you will not be able to see him. At a later date, you will be given the opportunity to review the footage of his attempt for education purposes. The door behind you is now open."

"May we ask who made first contact?" Crowe asked.

"As I said," the man responded, "The door behind you is open. You three did a wonderful job. You should be very proud."

Mayes stood and walked towards the door. She forced herself not to consider the millions of ways she could be being deceived. She forced herself to focus on the beauty of the landscape and her own good decisions. Something told her that it was real.

M.P. Christy

M. P. Christy is a Florida based writer who enjoys gardening, art, and delving into new depths of nerdiness.

Love's Illusions

John pointed to a row of beer bottles when the woman behind the roll-away bar cart made eye contact. "I'll have the brown ale, please."

The bartender pried off the cap and John made sure she saw the two singles he stuffed into the oversize mug. She thanked him with a nod.

He felt out of place at these receptions, and hovered in the background while co-workers made it their mission to talk business with people he didn't know or want to deal with. His grey suit and five-and-a-half foot height allowed him to be one with the background. Let others play the game. It was all an act anyway, with a script of product, marketing and profit margins.

Tipping the brown bottle to his lips, John stole a sideways glance at the woman next to him. She inclined her Cosmo in John's direction and extended her hand. "Hi. My name's Ally."

He swallowed a mouthful of beer too quickly, singing his throat. "I'm John," he gasped, all vestiges of confidence evaporated. Why would this woman want to talk to him? Let alone reveal her name. His knees went limp when she returned his gaze. He gestured toward the center of the room, searching for an appropriate response. "Nice affair. Are you representing someone?"

Ally's head tilted to one side and there was a delay before she spoke. "I work for a company that develops logic protocols. Primarily robotics and video games." They drifted to a corner. "How about you? Are you a developer?"

The lilt in her voice, her piercing blue eyes tripped John's emotions like a row of dominos. Sweat trickled down his torso and his words turned gooey. "I'm a numbers cruncher. My company creates customer profiles using demographic and psychographic statistics."

She scanned the room. "That's intriguing. You make up people?"

"In a sense. Our clients take our models and develop marketing strategies."

"How do you know who's a real person, and who isn't? Do you ever feel like you're making a false perception? Creating an illusionary customer?"

"No, not really. There's no deception with what we're doing. The data is spot on. And, statistics are just numbers. The models are as real as our clients want them to be."

Ally swirled the remains of her Cosmo and scanned the room. It was close to seven and people were leaving. "I'd love to talk about this more. Would you join me for dinner? I know a great Cuban restaurant not far from here."

John placed his empty bottle on the corner of the bar. "That sounds great. I've never had Cuban food, but I'm willing to try it."

Overtones of cumin and cilantro mingled with salsa music when they entered the restaurant. Their conversation continued over *picadillo* and black beans and rice.

"So, John, I think I hear you saying that because computers don't have personalities they can't act like humans. The computer only gives an impression of being a person."

"I guess so." Her smile, her voice, the music and the aromas from the kitchen interfered with his logical mind. "Numbers are essentially neutral and their meaning only seen through our perceptions."

A furrow separated her eyebrows. "I've always felt that a computer is basically a numbers cruncher. You crunch numbers and you are human. Can your laptop claim to be human. Have a personality?"

"Interesting question. Computers have quirks, but I'm not sure I can call that personality."

Ally settled into the burgundy vinyl of the booth. She gazed past John. "Let me tell you a little bit about me. I was in a horrible car accident. I woke up to a new leg, reconstructed face, and some new internal organs. It took years of rehab, physical therapy and multiple surgeries before I could function on my own.

John hunched forward. “That’s terrible. Are you OK now?”

“Yes, pretty much. The doctors worked miracles, just to save my life. It helped that my father was a military surgeon at a base in the Arizona desert.”

“Wow. You’re fortunate.”

Ally placed her arms on the table and cradled her merlot with both hands. “I don’t talk about it. I make a joke, the car was totaled, but I went to the body shop and got new parts.”

John rested his hand on hers. The unexpected coolness of her sent a shiver down his spine.

“I really feel something with you. A vibe or an energy.” John hunched himself closer to the table. “What’s that all about?”

“Yeah, I feel it too. It’s like an electric current when you touched my hand.”

“I have a confession to make,” John said. “I haven’t felt so close to another person for years. I don’t have girlfriends and I don’t go out. I’m uncomfortable around women. But you’re totally different. I feel there’s something growing between us.”

Ally sat back in the booth. The last notes of the band faded. “So do you think it’s a real feeling? Or is it because we’re here, in this restaurant with the music, the food, the drinks? Is it all about the scene we’re in?”

“You make it sound like we’re in a play or a movie.” John mimicked Ally and sat back. A sweep of his arm took in the restaurant. “I’m not going to accept that. All this is real. You’re real. And, my feelings toward you are real.”

Ally pushed aside her dessert plate and leaned forward until their foreheads nearly touched.

“There’s something else you need to know.” Her blue-on-blue eyes bore into his soul. “I also had brain damage. Essentially, the doctors rebuild and replaced my brain.”

“Whoa, Wait a minute. They replaced your brain? They can they do that?”

“Let’s say I’m an experiment. A military medical project. They gave me artificial intelligence so I could think and perform nearly all human functions. But they couldn’t program feelings or memories.”

John was at a loss. Brain damaged? Artificial intelligence? But she’s so real, so easy to talk to. “What’s it like?”

“I lost all memories. My history before the accident is a mystery. And I lack human emotions.”

“How does that make a difference?”

Ally shifted in her seat. “I don’t know compassion, empathy, or even love. But I’m learning. I don’t know if I’m human, or an enhanced robot. I ask myself, ‘Is this life only an illusion to further science?’ “

John reached across the table and took Ally's hand in both of his. "You're right in one sense. Because you can't hold love, so it is an illusion. But your life is real. There's nothing make believe about that."

"Thanks, John. That's sweet. I feel like I'm real. As real as AI can be."

"Forget about the AI. Love has to grow and evolve to become real."

Ally reached across the table and clutched his hands in hers. "Will you show me what love is?"

John studied her perfect face, caressed her hands and looked deep into her eyes. "Of course I will. Illusion or not, I know this is real."

William Clapper

William Clapper is a retired journalist writing from his home in Bradenton.

SPACE BAR

Heat scorched me as I picked my way through massive boulders and cactus. My destination was a homestead owned by a man named Lizard. Rivulets of sweat soaked my shirt. Lizard, leading the way, appeared dry and comfortable.

An hour earlier, while driving to San Diego from Yuma for a job interview with a regional magazine, I spotted what looked like small flying saucers on a frontage road. A hand-lettered sign read: Lizard's Flying Saucer Retrieval and Repair Service. Three bubble-topped space-craft sat on a flatbed trailer next to the sign. Thinking this might offer material for a freelance story in case I didn't get the magazine job, I exited the freeway to get a closer look. Slipping my reporter's notebook and a pen into my pocket, I stepped out of the car and leaned in to examine the saucers.

"Can I hep you?"

Startled, I swung around. The smiling owner of the 'Texas twang' wore faded coveralls and large green alien-themed sunglasses. His shoes were cobbled together from cowboy boot tops and worn-out sneakers. He radiated boheme.

"We git a few visitors here, sum them curious about them saucers, sum jist lost and sum with car problems from the mountain grade. Which is chew?

I smiled. "Just one of the curious,"

Lizard told me his name and talked about his flying saucer business. I played along with his 'shtick' then wondered if he was delusional. San Diego's backcountry is full of eccentric yet harmless characters.

We chatted for a few more minutes. Lizard invited me to see his homestead and the 'space bar' he ran for alien customers.

"Jist fruit juice and water, you understand. Them aliens can't hold their licker."

I laughed. "Lead the way."

We hiked about a quarter of a mile to a sign reading Space Bar. Underneath the sign lay a plank resting across two rocks. A jar of jerky and a Styrofoam cooler containing bottled water and juices sat on the plank. I gave him a dollar for water and wiped my face with a bar rag he offered.

"Thanks, do you get many visitors here?"

"Naw," said Lizard. "Jist CIA types dropping in to take occasional soil samples and, of course, my alien clients.

Playing along, I made an inane comment about meddlesome government types.

"Well," said Lizard. "I do know better than to tell them about the portal."

"The portal?"

"Yep, how you think them aliens git here from another galaxy? Wanna see it?"

Amused, I followed him to some boulders that hid a small cave.

"Go on, take a look," Lizard trailed me.

As I stepped up into the cave opening, my elbow struck and dislodged Lizard's sunglasses. I turned to apologize. The words died in my throat, and my bowels loosened when I saw the yellow glow of his cruel, reptilian eyes. I heard a strange sucking sound and landed in what I can only describe as a white void. Lizard's laughter rang in my ears.

***

I've no idea how long I've been here or why I'm still alive. Writing down what happened in my notebook provides a momentary distraction. Besides, if someone finds it later, my words will serve as a warning.

There are no exits in the void, only piles of clothing scattered throughout. I'm desperately thirsty. The air is hot and dry, like a dehydrator. Terror grips me as I recall the jar of jerky on the bar and that lizards are carnivores. My screams go unanswered.

Danielle Cook

Danielle Cook is a published writer, mixed media artist, and adventurer who recently relocated to Winter Garden from Palm Springs, California. After a career in Marketing, she retired and began writing short stories. She is now working on her first novel in the blended Science Fantasy genre.

In the Hospital (Again)

After I was stabbed in the gut, blood stained my shirt and ran down my pants. I tried to hide it, but the blood was obvious. A nurse found me and saved my life. There was something familiar about the nurse, but if she knew me, she kept it to herself. Unless my disguise as Guthrie slipped, everyone would think I was a struggling student.

The nurse insisted on taking me to the hospital. She picked one in the slum because it was close and I look like a young student with bad credit and no insurance. I'd spent a lot of time in hospitals over the years and didn't like them. I knew vampires would take my blood. Doctors would test new deadly drugs on me and wouldn't let me leave until they were done. This time was no different. I wanted to escape, but the chance never came. I survived, and they released me after a few days. It sounds incredible, but here's my story. If my mom says anything differ-ent, ignore her. She's tired from staying up late and worrying.

***

"Help! Is anybody there? Someone drained my blood. There is a puncture wound in my arm." The small wound didn't hurt, but I was concerned because it happened while I slept. An IV still flowed into the vein on the back of my left hand. Since I couldn't remember events from the previous night, I worried an enemy used that IV to add a knockout drug.

I assumed the IV pumped me up with something to keep the knife wound in my abdomen from killing me. The vein poked out and hurt. I wondered if the IV also rehydrated me from the blood the vampire took.

The nurse finally entered my room. "Mr. Guthrie, you don't need to panic. Our local vampire visited you last night for a blood sample. You're still on strong antibiotics. Since you can't eat, we're giving you a little extra in the IV to keep up your strength. You'll be here a few days. Is there a someone you want me to call?"

I couldn't believe she admitted that a vampire was taking my blood. There wasn't anybody to call, but I wanted my phone. At least the secret Guthrie persona was holding. If it failed, my situation would become dire. "Sorry, but without my cell I don't remember anybody's number. If you give me my cell for a few minutes, I'll take care of it." I hoped they'd believe my ruse and return the phone. I didn't want the nurse to know, but to me that phone was essential.

"My name is Sarah, and I'll be your night nurse until you get better. I'll see what they did with your phone and other belongings, but your mom probably took them with her."

Drifting off, I thought the nurse was friendly but confused. Mom was nowhere near there.

***

I woke up to a new day with a bad taste in my mouth and another puncture wound. No sense in calling for help. The vampire had the run of the hospital. My vein continued to hurt as the burning fluid from the IV poisoned my body. I hoped they'd finish dumping poisons into me and I could go home.

The white board said Hi, I'm Nurse Amanda. "Are you sure you want to be called Mr. Guth-rie? Johnnie has such a nice sound. You seem young to be a Mr. Guthrie." Something about nurse Amanda was curious. When I thought it over, it became obvious Amanda and the night nurse Sarah could be twins. I wondered if they were sisters or clones. Perhaps something more danger-ous was happening, but if so, I couldn't figure it out.

"Nurse Amanda, did anybody find my phone?"

"I haven't seen it, but is there somebody we can call for you? You have a phone by the bed, and the operator will help."

I wondered why they wouldn't return the phone. It made no sense. Did they think I was a kid, or had they lost it? "I don't really want to call anybody, but is it OK to go to the bathroom?" I had no real urgency, but I could think better someplace private and quiet.

"Sure, sweetie, let me untangle your cords, and you can wheel the IV into the bathroom. If you want to go for a walk after, that's OK."

I walked the halls looking for the best way to escape, but my injuries got the best of me. Rest was the only cure. Once in the bed I quickly fell asleep. Sleep came so fast I would later wonder if they were drugging me to keep me from escaping.

***

The nurse startled me as she came in. "Good morning, Mr. Guthrie. Good news. Your mom was here earlier, and you'll get released tonight." I wondered if I should say something about my mom. She hadn't been around for a long time. Anyway, I was too old for her to be in charge of me. It occurred to me that if my mom had come she would never have left without waking me to say hi. Well, it was probably best to play along with whatever was going on until I could get out of there.

I noticed the wound in my gut didn't hurt. When I felt the area, the hole had healed. Not quite a miracle, but surprising. "Nurse, did that vampire visit me last night?" I suspected the vampire saliva caused it to heal quickly.

"Yes, he visited you last night, and your blood looks fine. Did he wake you? Usually people don't wake when he takes their blood."

"He didn't wake me." It bothered me when I slept through his visit, but it seemed best to keep that information to myself. I thought about exploring, but I found myself drifting. Once again something put me to sleep.

"Son, wake up. It's time to go home. Are you feeling better?"

"Mom, I'm ready. It's no fun being in the hospital when you are eight. Thanks for playing along. Believing I was older and undercover was a lot of fun. I'm making plans for my next stay. I wish you'd let me have my phone."

"You're kinda weird, kid, but I'm glad that made it easier. You know the rules. No phone in bed. You have books and other games. There are two new rules. Next time don't tell the staff I'm not around, and don't pretend I'm a nurse. Also, don't give me two parts. Playing the day and night nurse was OK, but being called by two different names was confusing."

"OK, I'll write you into my next scenario but won't make you play multiple roles. The nurses yelled at me for changing their names on the whiteboard. I won't do it again, but I'm keeping the vampire. Pretending the guy drawing my blood was a vampire was great. When he found out I was pretending he was a vampire, he didn't even turn the lights on to take the blood sample. I wish we never had to come back, but thanks, Mom, for making it easier."

Michael Cox

Michael grew up in New Mexico and lived in Maryland and Germany before retiring in Florida. After years of writing dry engineering documentation, he decided to try his hand at writing fiction. He hopes it is more engaging than an engineering manual.

INSANITY

We stay six feet apart—isolated—
wanting to connect. Tick-tock.
Like me, the virus waits. We're time bombs.

Governors say, "Stay inside to stay alive."
Doctors, nurses, couriers emerge as heroes.
Invisible foe looms as death count mushrooms.

We hoard toilet paper, stock up on food
to eat alone, check our temperatures,
and watch frightening news. The curtain's

down on Broadway and Major League
Baseball's out. Down and out—home alone,
my inner voice shouts, "You don't deserve to live!"

In seclusion. No kind voice argues.
I need a lover to lean on. Others seek
scapegoats. Fear leads to stranger-danger

warnings. Virus threatens and cruel con
artists create illusions meant to scam Gram.
Detained, distanced, warned—

a plague on all our houses.
In exile, my inner voice repeats,
"You don't deserve to live."

We must flatten the curve—sanitize.
Cooperate—in this together, unraveling—
on edge—worn like a threadbare collar.

When we go outdoors, we don bandanas
suitable for bandits—social distancing.
Autonomy's an artifice. We need others.

Alone in the milky night, I emerge
from my sea of isolation. I'm a driftwood
ghost from a shipwreck, going with the flow.

Adrift without ties, my inner demons emerge.
Coping, but solitude's unbearable. Frantic—
I'm a queen bee in need of a colony.

I seek the vicarious love and fantasy
found in steamy romance-novel pages.
In the time of the deadly coronavirus, I open

a book for my happy-ever-after ending.
That's what books are for—transcending.

Melody Dimick

Melody Dean Dimick, winner of three Royal Palm literary awards from the Florida Writers Association and two Excellence in the Arts awards from the Daytona Writers Guild, is the current president of the Florida Writers Foundation. She and her husband Barry love concerts, pinochle, pickleball, and attending conferences together.

PERSPECTIVE

Come see.
I have a collection of things made small
for ease of handling.
Time, for instance.
A state of mind really,
managed from Greenwich.
Not infinite, is it, if I can be late?
Highly complicit in "Chinese Water Torture."
Horrifying, when contemplating one's days in hell.
Or heaven, if you ask me.
Pity any three-year-old who hears "soon" or "later."
Quantifiable, if you can bear
watching water work its way through stone.

My grandfather's pocket watch,
there on the walnut table,
opens at the push of a button
and has for ninety years.
But even closed, its black hands keep time.
Keep time—for each day I slavishly wind it.
Held to the ear, the watch is alive.
You can hear it, feel it—tick.
Time goes on.
Grouching along with a cane and a pipe.

There is an antique globe beside it.
All the world at the time.
Ancient cartographers did the best they could
when information was scarce,
giving mariners fair warning:

"Beyond here, there be dragons."
Wrap a map around a sphere and see what happens.
You walk around in circles.
Tectonic plates slide and crash.
The globe is rife with possibility.
Things might be different with a second twirl.
But no, there it is again—Mozambique.

And here stands a bonsai.
A perfect tree in a summer light,
rooting its way into crusty earth and moss.
Dwarfing the small clay figure
of the Chinese gentleman at its feet.
It makes a mockery of near and far.
I wish it would keep its distance,
so I could walk there to stand in its shade.
But the closer I get, the lesser the tree.
If I can't hang a swing from that lowest branch,
what will become of summer?

Betsy Donohue

Betsy moved to Florida from Maryland six years ago and has become a member of several writing groups. She is inspired by the many talented writers she has met in Florida. Poetry is her first love, but she also writes juvenile and adult fiction.

Billy and the Time Machine

Dr. William Masters twirled the dials.

His assistant, Jason, said, "Are you ready, Dr. Masters?"

Masters glanced at the helmet dangling above his head. "Jason, if this works, it could be the most significant discovery in human history. And, yeah, I'm ready." He closed his eyes and turned his thoughts to the experiment. This was his chance to change the past.

Billy Masters sat next to his father in their brand new pickup, bright red and without a single dent. The ride to school would be short. He craned his head to catch glimpses of the road ahead, thankful for the bumps, each giving him a fleeting glance over the dash.

"How do you like it, son?"

"It's great, dad. Smells good, too."

"Tighten up that seat belt. Wouldn't want you popping out before we get to school."

They laughed. He remembered the laugh. It was then that something yellow burst into view from his father's side of the truck. A squeal of grinding metal filled the cabin. Shoulder straps bit into Billy's neck as brilliant shards of glass turned into a slow motion ice storm. And the world rolled.

Seconds later —no engine sound, no laughter, just the pounding beat of his heart.

A blur of white coats, blue coats, pulled at him, mumbling words he couldn't understand. He awoke in the hospital. His mom cried.

Jason said, "I have to admit that I'm worried for you."

"Don't fret. It'll all be over in a few minutes."

The time has come to change the past.

Jason said, "I've started up the backup generators."

"Excellent. You've been a great help, Jason."

His assistant blushed. "I know we've been over this, Dr. Masters, but this trip of yours still feels like a paradox."

"Paradoxes are illusions."

"So, what do you think will happen?"

"Lots of theories, few facts. First off, the only thing going into the past is my consciousness. It's not like my body will go back. That would end up making a mess, especially if I run into myself." Masters forced out a chuckle, more to relax himself than Jason.

"Yeah, but you'll end up in your brain … your past brain, right?"

"That's what should happen."

"And that would mean that a younger you—."

"Will get a visitor … inside his head."

In time to save my father.

Jason fiddled with the helmet. "Well, do you remember something like that happening?"

"No, I don't."

"Right there is a paradox."

"You're over-thinking it. Maybe I've forgotten the whole thing. Or after I come back, that's when I'll remember."

"I still don't get it."

"Picture reality as a stack of movie frames, each one representing a point in time. As your consciousness moves through those frames, you become aware of each one. The direction of movement is how we sense time. All I'm doing is going in reverse."

"Then why not go forward … you know, to the future? That sounds like it would be more fun."

"You're assuming my future exists. What if I die tomorrow? Remember, I need to be alive to make a visit to myself. At least I'm sure the past exists."

Besides that's where my father died.

"Let's get on with it."

Jason finished adjusting the helmet with its myriad wires. "I've got you set for September 13, 1999 at 7:30 AM local time, is that right?"

"Don't forget to yank me back in precisely ten minutes."

"What if that doesn't work … I mean the yanking?"

"Then I'll be stuck in a time loop."

Masters tensed at the thought—living as little Billy, reaching his present age, then going back again, and again, for the rest of eternity.

At least wouldn't know it was happening.

"Damn."

"Damn is right." Masters shook off the tension and gave Jason the thumbs up. He felt the helmet vibrate. With a flash of light the movie began running backwards. Image after image flittered by—drinking beer in a college dorm room, snow gathering on a window sill, making love on a stretch of beach, the high school graduation ceremony with mom waving a kerchief, seventh grade during recess when he got punched in the nose, the bitter cold while dropping flowers on a casket.

***

"Ow!"

"Are you all right, dear?" His mother loomed into view. "Hurry and finish your breakfast. Your father's warming up the truck. You don't want to be late on your first day of school."

"Just got a headache is all."

His mother ran her fingers across his head. "No fever. Does it still hurt?"

"No." He gazed at his mom, fighting the urge to jump out of his seat and feel her warm embrace again.

"Finish up. I'll get your coat."

Billy looked up at the wall clock—7:30 AM.

I'm really here.

Ten minutes. He was having breakfast at home with both parents still alive. He longed to savor the moment, to make it last. The truck's engine roared to life outside. His father waited, not knowing that death lurked minutes away. Maybe all Billy had to do was stay out of the truck.

His mother came back into the kitchen. "Time to go." She slipped one arm at a time into his coat, and nudged his lunchbox closer. "There now."

"Mom. I'm not feeling too good."

"Nonsense. You're just nervous. You'll be fine." She whisked him off his chair, handed him the lunchbox and a backpack. "Don't keep your father waiting."

He felt himself being shoved out the door. The brisk cold air was scented with fallen leaves. The sight of the red pickup twisted his stomach.

Its passenger door swung open. "Get in, buddy. How do you like the new truck?"

He thought about the stacked movie frames.

What if I can't change them? What if all I can do is relive the worst moment of my life?

"Dad."

I don't remember the headache.

"That's it! My headache!"

"What?" The pickup jerked forward. "Get that seat belt on, buddy."

I didn't have a headache and that's not what you said.

In seconds his dad would be dead.

"Dad. Stop the truck!"

"What's the problem?"

He screamed. "Stop, now!"

His dad pulled over to the side of the road as a yellow van appeared out of nowhere and skidded in front of them, crashing nose first into the ditch alongside.

"Holy mackerel. You okay, buddy?" His father jumped out and ran to the van.

The dashboard clock read 7:41 AM.

I'm still here.

A beat later dad was back. "The driver's okay."

Billy said, "All this was supposed to happen."

"What are you talking about, son?"

What if a second stack of movie frames exists?

"I was supposed to come back."

His dad looked pale. "Son, I think we're both playing hooky today."

Billy's life as an adult blurred like the ephemeral details of a dream upon awakening.

"I'm so happy I'm here with you, dad."

"So am I, buddy."

***

"Ow!"

"Are you all right, dear?" His mother loomed into view. "Hurry and finish your breakfast. Your father's warming up the truck. You don't want to be late on your first day of school."

Arthur M. Doweyko

Arthur is a world-renown scientist who shares the 2008 Thomas Alva Edison Patent Award for the discovery of a new anti-cancer drug. In addition to authoring award-winning science fiction novels and short stories, he teaches chemistry at the Indian River State College, writes an edgy blog, and paints in oils.

THE BANK BRANCH

"Wealth and security are illusions, perhaps so too are people and institutions."

***

On a sunny day in the late Fall of 1968, Miss Fiona Entwistle looked across the street from Sunnyvale's front windows. "We certainly can use a bank around here," she chirped. "It is so far down to University Crossing when I have to deposit my annuity check or an occasional present from my son, Gabriel. Now, I won't have to take that smelly bus." She pinched her ancient nose at the memory of her last bus ride.

"Yep, real convenient," added septuagenarian Frank Gershwin, who liked to have a few bucks in his wallet on Poker Night. "Not to mention a place to deposit my Social Security check."

The residents of the Sunnyvale Retirement Home were almost universal in their appreciation of the new bank branch recently opened across the street. The refurbished building featured a large lighted "First National" sign over the door and was festooned inside and out with "FDIC" stickers. The elderly residents joyfully read the signs to each other as they waited; "Each depositor insured by the US Government to at least $25,000."

The bank building had been a run-down neighborhood grocery store, but now featured three tellers' windows and two desks in dark wood. The interior sported calming gray paint and soft blue carpeting. Large wall posters trumpeted the benefits of the bank's mortgages and home equity loans; of course, the residents of Sunnyvale no longer purchased homes or owned any houses with equity for them to borrow against.

What they did have was a steady flow of checks to deposit into healthy checking and savings accounts. While Social Security checks in 1968 averaged only a few hundred dollars, the monthly flow deposited into the branch from Sunnyvale alone was over thirty thousand. The Sunnyvale residents were quick to avail themselves of the "First National Bank and Trust," a name of financial rectitude if ever there was one.

Geraldine Engel was the new branch manager. Prior to opening day, she visited the home and talked to the Sunnyvale residents about the proud 123-year history of "FNBT," as she referred to it. "We've been serving our communities forever," she proudly stated. Miss Engel assured one and all she was a serious career banker and "was married to my job."

"Such a nice lady," Clarice remarked to Miss Fiona over that afternoon's tea, hosted by the bank. Although the bank's Miss Engel was a little stout and wore a fair amount of face powder, today she was smartly attired in a Chanel-type lilac suit and hat "Jackie Kennedy would surely just love."

Ivy, one of the home attendants, nodded in agreement as she slid another scone from the table into her smock pocket for later.

When the Sunnyvale residents or their elderly neighbors visited the branch, Miss Engel or Mr. Finchley, who sat at the two desks in the front, would serve them coffee and Miss Engel's "homemade" shortbread while the customers waited in comfortable chairs.

"How are you, Mr. Hellman? How's your grandson; he still the star of his Little League team?" Sunnyvale's residents felt they were banking with new friends; all except grumpy Harald Grosen, and he banked with his son downtown anyways.

The bankers would take the customers' deposits up to the teller windows. There, "young Mr. Getchell" or "pretty Miss Fortnum" stamped the checks and returned their deposit receipts printed on flimsy paper. Often, they could barely make out the printed amount or date, but the typed account statements on First National stationery arrived promptly at the beginning of each month.

Three months after the branch opened, an odd incident occurred when Henry Wallace brought in his nephew to co-sign an auto loan for him. Neither Miss Engel nor Mr. Finchley could find the right loan application form. After apologizing, Mr. Finchley asked Mr. Wallace and his nephew to come back later in the week when they could get a loan application from the main office. When they returned, the incipient borrowers filled out what looked to be a photocopied application; Henry's nephew noted the "First National Bank & Trust" header didn't look quite straight.

One Wednesday a few weeks later, when Frank Gershwin went to get twenty dollars for the game at the Elks, the branch was closed. Frank told his table he couldn't get to the bank and threw down an IOU. The other five at his table looked away in embarrassment for him.

Then Miss Fiona's check, donating to the Methodist Church's campaign for a new piano, bounced! "Why, that's impossible," she huffed, waving her statement around like a fan.

Led by Miss Fiona, residents hurried across the street to pull their money from the branch. They started knocking on the door on Wednesday; were camped out in front early the next day, and, by Friday, the residents had made calls to their lawyers, as well as their congressman in Washington.

Mr. Hellman's call to the FDIC revealed that "The federal insurance company had no record of a 'First National Bank and Trust' in Monroe County." The call the residents couldn't bring themselves to make was to their grown children.

No one was surprised when the branch doors were chained and padlocked the following Monday. Miss Fiona had tears in her eyes; "seven-thousand, three-hundred and ten dollars, and sixty-two cents," she kept muttering to no-one in particular.

Frank lost his desire to play poker. Without his savings, he worried constantly whether his monthly Social Security check would cover his room and board at Sunnyvale, his home for the last six years. Ten months after the branch closed, when costs at the home exceeded the amount of his Social Security check, he walked out the door, and proceeded to cross the nearby train tracks in front of the 9:30 Downtown Express.

The residents stopped leaving the home. If that building across the street wasn't a bank, what else wasn't real out there. Was that a policeman, or someone dressed up to take advantage of old people like themselves? How did they know that the nice Revered Peasley, who visited Sunnyvale regularly, even attended divinity school?

For that matter, who were they? Miss Entwistle no longer believed she was previously a dynamic fifth-grade teacher; she feared she might just be one more stupid old woman. Perhaps uppity Henry Wallace really hadn't owned the Wallace Ford dealership on the edge of town; he could have learned about all those different cars from magazines. And new President Nixon, well, he didn't look anybody's idea of a real President. Not handsome like President Kennedy, or forceful like that foul-mouthed LBJ.

The residents of the home went into a rapid decline. Just two years later, the few remaining residents of Sunnyvale were moved to the County Home for the Elderly; Sunnyvale was out of business. Harald, pushing his walker along, was led to the dilapidated rented bus, sitting on the street midway between Sunnyvale and the old bank branch. The bus would take them across town to their new home. As he boarded the bus, Ivy heard him mutter, "It was that damn bank, that's what killed this place."

Bob Ellis

Bob Ellis has lived and worked on three continents and swum in all the oceans of the world! A retired financial services exec and consultant, Bob now resides in SWFL where he writes, boats, gardens, and writes some more.

MOON FLYING

Her arms moved at one point, but for the life of her, she now couldn't swing them more than a bit in each direction. A squeak, a groan, and her arms unbent a little more.

Forget her legs. They might as well have been made of sticky rice mortar.

She gave her hands an experimental squeeze. Her fingers closed on empty air. Yet her nose discovered the air wasn't empty, after all. A rich, meaty scent drifted past her nostrils at intervals, almost overwhelming the gentler floral scent that stirred memories of past—what? Past meals? Strolls through a garden? Her unmoving tongue savored braised beef stew seasoned with ginger and anise. Her practiced nose recalled the brazen scent of peach blossoms. These memories rose in her mind, faded, as if they had been left out in the rain. As if they were not hers.

What could she see? Were her eyes even open? Perhaps she had never closed them. Her eyes, unblinking, gazed upon the flickering of candles painted across translucent cloth, like light made solid. In her mind's eye, the moon rose full and ripe above her head.

Her name swam into her thoughts, sluggish as it wrestled into focus: Chang E. Everything else remained indefinite. Her entire life until then spooled behind her in a bright, unbroken ribbon, as blank as the surface of an egg. Without the feel of grass or earth under her feet, her soul drifted in an unseen wind.

Up to this moment, curiosity shaped Chang E's thoughts. Curiosity tinged with a hint of resolve. But now, fear stole into her awareness on cat's paws. Without the ability to see danger, move herself a meaningful amount, even remember more than her name, she was vulnerable to anyone or anything wishing her harm. A new urgency forced her head a little downward. She stared.

Below her chin, Chang E's body stretched, paper-thin and full of holes, some in the pattern of flowers and clouds. Arms, legs, and torso shone in painted shades of red and yellow and blue.

She was not even a whole person.

Her mind raced with questions. Who was she? Was she real? What was her purpose?

While these panicked thoughts surfaced, one after the other, the scent of stew and the flicker of candlelight continued to press on her consciousness. She rubbed her fingers together. The faint rasp of scraped leather reached her ears. What kind of magic was this?

If she moved too much, she might draw attention to herself. Doing so was dangerous when she didn't know who was nearby. Yet the sights and sounds and smells around her filled her heart with longing. The temptation to seek clues about her situation pulled at her desire to learn more about her surroundings. Stay silent and still, or explore around her? In that instant, she could not decide which path to follow.

A drumming, rapid as a startled heartbeat, thumped by her head. She jerked. Her arms and legs swung in every direction. Even now, she could not control them. Her limbs collapsed as she moved up, up, up.

Moments later, her body pressed against the translucent cloth she had seen earlier. Her arms stretched in front of her in a gesture of supplication, but she felt no such emotion. Confusion and fear swelled as her body moved on its own.

That was it. She would find out who she was, cost her what it would, even if that cost was her life. With a last, monumental effort, she forced her body away from the cloth so that she could see, feel, sense anything. Anything at all.

In one smooth gesture, Chang E's body flipped around, and she gazed upon the blazing intensity of ten suns. Below her, a small, flat rabbit danced on a thin rod of bamboo. The drums stopped, and the haunting strains of an erhu swirled around her in a storm of song.

With the first notes from the narrow, stringed instrument, Chang E's mind flooded with sights, sounds, smells, tastes, textures. Memories. The feel of tender fingers, dabbing paint in tiny strokes on her leather body. The scent of home-cooked stew prepared by mothers for their beloved children. The sound of laughter as Chang E danced for her audience, arms akimbo. And the sight of that audience gazing upon her with amusement and astonishment.

Who was she? A shadow puppet, a thespian sharing stories of inspiration that add color to ordinary days.

Was she real? She was as real as the performers helping her dance at the end of her rods. Her memories were their memories. And their memories were hers.

What was her purpose?

Chang E paused in her train of thought, even as she bowed at the end of a rod. She had asked the question in a moment of fear, searching for the universe to give her purpose. Now, with her fear gone, her purpose grew within her. No longer was her life as uncontrollable as her body. No longer must she wait for the universe to give her an answer. She could decide her purpose for herself.

The notes of the erhu became soft and plaintive. She had a past. And she knew her future. But right now, what was important was the present. The members of her audience waited for her next move. She intended to give them a show they would never forget.

What kind of magic was this? Only the magic infused in endless rediscovery of who she was, of the purpose she chose.

The ten suns blazing in the sky faded away. A silver moon rose in their place. The audience members gasped as Chang E's arms swung freely, reaching for the moon.

Jessie Erwin

As a registered dietitian nutritionist, Jessie finds food and cooking often appear in her writing. She writes middle grade fiction and picture books, raises two kids, and can make a mean chocolate date cake.

Harmy

Harland gentlemanly rested his hand on Tammy's waist, the way the ballroom dance instructor had demonstrated—not too close to her bra strap, nor too near her derrière. This required skill as his hands were large and her torso was short.

After thirty years of marriage, they still danced like this. Harland believed wanderin' hands and lips belonged behind closed doors.

When Harland retired as postmaster of their tiny town, the couple celebrated by renting a houseboat. They would have three months of quality time alone, drifting aimlessly downriver.

Tammy planned to paint miniature nature scenes. Harland would reread his collection of cowboy novels and organize his modest stamp collection. Tammy thought he should be sick of stamps, but it was his only hobby besides Saturday night dances at the Moose lodge. Harland said the Fox Trot and the Cha-Cha were plenty of exercise. His heart doctor disagreed.

They paid the non-refundable rental in advance. The company allowed them to name their houseboat for the duration. After choosing from a pile of wooden letters, they laughed as they spelled the same name—Harmy. Like teenagers, Tammy and Harland slid the mash-up of their names into a Lucite frame they would attach to the boat.

The couple took the waterproof instruction booklet home and read it from cover to cover. For a full week, they gathered and packed supplies.

Harland spent an entire evening deciding what Louis L'Amour titles to bring on the journey: *Where Buzzards Fly, Ride the Dark Trail, Long Ride Home.* When Harland lifted the box of books, he felt a familiar pain in his chest. He'd get it checked at the end of the summer. Surely, the rest and relaxation would cure all their ills—Tammy's eczema, and Harland's persistent toe fungus. He'd go barefoot all day.

***

After pushing away from shore, Tammy checked the fire extinguisher and examined life jackets. The bell was to be used sparingly as the ringing disturbed wildlife. She said, "Harland. It says here," she tapped page six of the safety manual, "from sunset to sunrise there must be white lights eight feet above the water so other boats can see us for a mile."

Tammy knew Harland wouldn't respond. He was on the upper deck wiggling his toes in the morning sun. She tested the light and the switch, making sure everything was ship-shape, a term she used when spring cleaning her house.

***

A week into the trip, Tammy worried that Harland didn't bring enough books, although she never heard him complain.

For Harland's retirement, his post office colleagues gifted him two fishing poles. He was eight years old the last time he cast a line. He caught a cold, not a trout. Tammy had joked that they could sit side-by-side all summer catching nothing.

The houseboat rocked as water lapped at its sides. Tammy imagined Harland being lulled to sleep in the deck chair on the roof. She hated to wake him. "Harland?" Tammy thought she heard her husband snort. "Harland, honey?" Tammy put her foot on the first stair leading to the next level. "Hamburgers or pork chops?"

Cooking was a pleasure in the small but well-stocked galley. Tammy had learned to make chicken chili, and cornbread in a skillet. She left a buttered piece of warm bread for a snoring Harland. Fifteen minutes later, the plate was clean. Tammy hoped the gulls hadn't eaten Harland's snack.

The marauding seagulls were relentless, always trying to snatch a wriggling fish from her line. Tammy learned to throw apple peels or stale crackers as far away from the boat as possible to divert their attention. One day, she wrestled a five-pound bass from a determined bird. Harland didn't care for fish, but she fried it alongside his favorite country-style potatoes.

Tammy turned the sizzling pork chop. "Smell that Harland?"

***

After a month, river-living had roused dormant artistic inspiration in Tammy. She painted red-winged blackbirds, and cattails that looked like corn dogs on long sticks. One afternoon, a milkweed butterfly landed on Tammy's wrist, her paintbrush in mid-air. She and the butterfly didn't move for three minutes. That was when she realized the stubborn scaly rash in the crook of her arm had disappeared. Harland was right. The sun and fresh air had cured some of their ills.

One morning, Tammy watched a fluffy sheep-of-a-cloud separate into snowballs. She wanted to paint the forever-changing formations. When she finally removed her gaze from the sky, she realized the scenery in front of her had remained the same. She laughed. "Harland, honey!" Tammy wondered if she heard Harland stirring in his deck chair. "You won't believe it! We forgot to pull up anchor!"

Tammy didn't wait for Harland to come down. She'd let him rest.

How many years had Harland woken at dawn to adhere to the unofficial creed of the Postal Service? Neither snow, rain, heat, etc. And Harland had always come home for lunch. Tammy was often covered in paint, a smudge of gesso streaked across her cheek. She'd wash her hands and heat canned tomato soup and grill cheese sandwiches. Back then, Tammy painted all day, hoping to profit from her landscapes. Harland was proud of her talent and hung a watercolor of wildflowers in the lobby of the post office.

Tammy walked up the stairs and stood on the roof landing. She shielded her eyes from the blinding sun. "Time to push off," she said. Harland looked handsome in his flannel shirt and Levi's. Or was he wearing shorts? He was barefoot to be sure. Tammy descended the stairs. "No need to come down. I'm getting good at this."

The pole dug into the thick loam of the shore. Tammy watched minnows dart through the water trying to escape her unpredictable thrusts. The boat turned slowly yet easily compared to the first time. She wondered if the owner would sell the houseboat to her. The name *Harmy* would be permanent, not replaced by the next occupant.

In the early evening, Tammy went up to the roof. Her pink flowered dress undulated in the breeze. The aluminum flooring squeaked beneath her leather-heeled dance shoes. She closed the book of stamps—colorful trains, ships, and all modes of travel—significant to Harland, but of no actual value. Tammy placed the magnifying glass, the aluminum perforation gauge, and the round tongs into the cloth pouch. She pushed play on the cassette player they bought for their first anniversary. Eric Clapton sang, 'Wonderful Tonight.'

Tammy held out her hand to the empty chair. "Shall we dance?"

Kimberlee Esselstrom

Kimberlee writes true and imagined slice-of-life stories for all ages. She has been published in the Christian Science Monitor, Highlights for Children, FWA collections, and more. Her award-winning novel *Mischief Makers* is available on Amazon. Kimberlee loves to travel and always takes her writing on the road.

The Mirrors

Lovely girl of twelve peers in the mirror,
Sees horrid face.
Zits obscure skin's smooth reality.
She doesn't see beyond the temporary.
Hates her visage.
Fat, she thinks, though thin, in fact.
Her truth in the reflection.
Shattered image in her mind's eye.

Woman of ninety peers in the mirror,
Sees former face.
Through clouded eyes, wrinkles vanish,
Age spots fade, blush appears.
She sees beyond to memories
Of lovely skin and sparkling eyes.
Her truth in the reflection.
Enchanted image in her mind's eye.

The mirrors are silent, yet echo illusions,
Figments and glimpses of youth and age
Transformed by altered views.

Ann Favreau

Ann is a past president of the Suncoast Writers Guild. Her prose and poetry has appeared in FWA Magazines and several Collections. She loves to travel and takes her audiences with her when she shares her writing at local presentations.

A Serving of Winter Solstice

I wake once again
to harsh winter sounds
howling and whining
through vulnerable cracks and crevices.

I am angry
with this constant companion
of crushing cold
and growing gloom.

On this morning
I sit in the dining room
curtains parted
offering a view.

Birch trees sway
silvery and stark—
mesmerizing.

Icy, stratus clouds
vie for position
in front of
the pale-yellow orb.

Slivers of light
break through
and the outside
is brought to me.

There—
on my glass table
is my serving
of reflections.

The trees—
my silverware.

The sun—
an oversized pancake
glazed with silhouettes
of swirling, syrupy clouds.

Glistening, granules of snow—
fine as sugar
sprinkle themselves over
my contemplations.

On this morning
how can I remain angry
with such intriguing beauty?

Linda Feist

Linda relocated to sunny Florida from snowy Western New York. She has several published works, including stories in four Chicken Soup for the Soul books. Happily writing instead of shoveling snow, Linda's been an RPLA finalist a few times over. She hopes to one day receive an award.

Elusive Illusions

Pregnant at last—
dreams ran rampant.
Miscarried—twice.
The dreams died, too.

Pregnant again,
but afraid to dream.
A healthy baby boy—
the dreaming resumed.

At two – a seizure disorder
At four – still the "terrible twos"?
At six – it must be ADD.
At eight – a learning disorder

Years passed, dreams faded.
This once-precious bundle of joy,
this repository of hope for happiness
forged his own illusions.

At ten – auditory processing disorder
At twelve – a movement disorder
At fourteen – autism spectrum
Tackled one obstacle, another emerged.

At twenty-five – depression, anxiety
Without friends, unable to work—
how does he define each day
in an endless chain of emptiness?

At thirty – paranoia
At thirty-six – schizophrenia?
When did the illusions become delusions?
A lifetime of broken dreams and shattered illusions.

Chris Flocken

Chris Flocken graduated from the University of Maryland and Rollins College. She is currently working on a memoir and also writes short stories and poetry. Her poems have been published in the Florida State Poets Association's *Cadence* in 2017, 2018, and 2019. She lives in Orlando with her family.

Away From It All

The coffee gurgled and bubbled as it perked, the aroma drifting to where Jamie snuggled under a blanket, poring over her copy of *Little Women*, losing herself in the words of her favorite author. The fire crackled and popped, chasing away the midmorning chill, the pungent smell of burning wood mingling with the coffee, creating a cozy, warm feeling that bloomed in her middle.

Only when vacationing in the mountains did she take the time to grind the beans, then percolate the coffee, until the pot of rich liquid reached perfection.

Home. This felt like home.

In reality, her cabin in the Smoky Mountains was a vacation rental—not hers at all. But, for now, it felt like hers. Soon enough she'd buy her own dream home, just like this one.

***

"Doctor, how long can she remain like this?" the nurse asked.

The physician checked Jamie's neural inputs, a tangle of wires and silicon. All indicators pointed to success—a bioengineered success. Jamie would adjust… learn…as her software and hardware continued to mesh, becoming one—wetware.

"Theoretically, as long as her body and the new hardware hold out. Meanwhile, with her body, mind, and spirit freed from pain and anxiety, the disease attacking her can be more easily addressed. When the cure for her illness is formally tested and available, Jamie, now part machine, part human, will come out the other side of this, cured and healthy, if not altered somewhat."

The nurse adjusted the digital readout, tracking the output that documented Jamie's medical stats. The nurse nodded. "Vitals normal." She released a sigh, shaking her head. "Just imagine… Almost like a permanent vacation. I wonder where she is right now."

The doctor gave an easy laugh. "The software is self-propelled. Jamie is exactly where she wants to be and, most important, free of pain. All her pain receptors are overridden. Plus any disease-related stress is nonexistent. In her world she's healthy. The absence of those negative influences could help her recovery as well."

"And should she need life support, what then?"

"Assuming that is Jamie's documented wish, she can remain safely nestled in her world, while the necessities of life are handled right here, in real time." The doctor raised his eyebrows. "Other questions?"

"Maybe later."

"All right. Let's tell the family the good news—their daughter is alive, comfortably awaiting treatment in her very own virtual reality."

***

Little white puffs of cloud hung in the air, dissipating with each step Jamie took farther up the mountain. With a little luck she'd reach the peak by noon, then would relax and enjoy the view before heading back down. Leaves mushed under her feet, their brilliant reds and vibrant yellows subdued but still partially visible, despite the lateness of the season, snatching the attention of anyone fortunate enough to catch their colorful parade. Flowering heather peeked out from under the light dusting of snow, dotting the meadow with their purple petals, confident in their bold stance as they reached toward the warming rays.

Perched on a rock, Jamie gave her attention to the expansive countryside below—a glimpse in time, a collage created of this moment. Tomorrow the landscape would appear subtly different. The leaves a hue deeper, the forest floor another layer higher, the air heavier perhaps. Today mattered, and the moments within each twenty-four-hour period came only once for everyone.

Breathtaking.

A noise jolted her, interrupting Jamie's thoughts. An animal maybe? Twisting and glancing side to side, nothing appeared out of the ordinary, but she stood from the rock and lifted her feet to check it out anyway.

A familiar tone… She paused, listening. Voices called to her—ones she remembered. Her breath heaved, while her heart raced.

Jamie, we're here.

"Mom? Dad? But no one knows of my place."

Come back to us, dear.

She swept her gaze across the expanse, searching. "Where?"

Pain seized her, its tendrils reaching out and cinching tight. Her breath caught as the landscape fractured, tumbling from her mind, like shards of broken glass. Before her eyes a kaleidoscope of color slid into a brilliant intensity of comingled hues, then washed away. *What's happening?* She circled in an empty void, the white haze left behind surrounding her. *What?*

Jamie arrived…somewhere.

Her eyelids fluttered, then opened, narrowing against the harsh glare in the unnatural light. Silently she studied the pair before her, familiar but different, her brain trying to make sense of what she instinctively knew to be true. "Mom, Dad, you're so different."

Her dad chuckled. "Fifteen years will do that to a person."

Jamie's eyes widened.

"That's right, dear," her mom added. "Take a look for yourself. But first prepare. This new body of yours has been working overtime to make you well."

Her mom placed a mirror in front of her daughter's face, adjusting the angle of reflection so Jamie had a complete view. She gasped. Odd tubing attached to her head, traveling down the side of her neck, where it connected to another array of metal, yet seemingly flexible, rods.

"Do you remember anything?" her mother asked.

A line furrowed between Jamie's eyes, deepening with her concentration. "I wasn't here…just now."

"Right, honey. But you are now." A warm hand squeezed hers. "And you're well, darling—healed." Her mom beamed at Jamie. "How about we talk with the doctor now?"

A tall man, his body marred with its own combination of tubing and wiring, scrutinized a digital readout beside her, before returning his focus to his patient.

A smile tugged his lips. "Welcome, Jamie, to 2040—the year ALS has finally met its match. You're one of the lucky ones. How about we discuss your new normal?"

J.W. Garrett

J.W. Garrett writes speculative fiction from the sunny beaches of Jacksonville, Florida. Currently, she is hard at work on the next book in her Realms of Chaos series, releasing August 2020. When she's not hanging out with her characters, her favorite activities are reading, running and spending time with family.

Jesus Ants

A week ago, I found an aggressive ant in my peony plants. I killed it just as I had slain armies like him in the past. I supply the healthiest, pest-free plants to my customers, even if it requires the extermination of a few bugs along the way.

That night I soaked in the bathtub. I had just rotated onto my belly and noticed that the caulk between the tile wall and porcelain had become black in some areas. Leaning on my elbows, I ran my right index finger along a two-inch line of sealant to see if it would rub off. At first, I thought it was a floater wiggling down my eye. That's when I saw actual movement, racing in like the cars in *Fast & Furious*. Ants. I had black ants funneling into my bathtub! I jumped up, naked and dripping, stepped out of the tub and slipped, clunking my left knee against the porcelain. I landed flat on my butt.

Immobilized on the ground, I watched, hypnotized, as three rows of walk-on-water Jesus Ants continued to launch themselves onto the soapy water. The next brigade climbed on top of them as the ones on the bottom formed a matted life raft. The ever-widening raft of comrades grew higher toward the tub's lip. Chills and pain finally broke the spell. I grabbed my towel and wrapped it around me.

The pest platoons continued their advance. If I didn't let the water out, they could climb over the tub's edge. I wasn't about to stick my arm into that sea of insects. Instead, I hobbled to the guest bedroom to retrieve a wire hanger to loosen the rubber drain plug.

If I could hook the ring on the stopper, I could yank it up.

"Got it!" I growled, "Die you bastards."

I ought to be in the Guinness Book of Records for the highest number of ant kills. Victory was mine that day.

I turned on the shower to hasten the ants' exit down the drain. Relieved at the sight of their disintegrating life raft, I limped to the garage to get ant spray and gloves. When I returned, the influx of ants had stopped. I secured the Velcro tight around the wrist of my gloves, drenched the tiny crevice with the poison, then stuffed toilet paper in it to avoid strays. My hermetically sealed gloved hands pushed the remaining stragglers swirling to their final home down the drain.

I traded my gloves for a robe and went to investigate the other side of the bathroom wall. It was a back porch of solid masonry. My flashlight revealed no entry point. I've heard of ants living inside walls, but that many was unnerving.

I applied ice to my knee and called my boyfriend for sympathy. He didn't seem too impressed by my creepy-crawly story. I'd been too busy defending my territory to document the attack with a selfie. He did volunteer to bleach the black line and re-caulk the gaps.

While on the phone, I noticed that my finger that had touched the moldy caulk was black, the entire finger. *Probably leftover dirt from inside my gardening glove*. After I hung up, I scrubbed my finger, but the black wouldn't budge.

Whatever. I need to take a Tylenol PM and get some sleep.

***

I dreamt that ants lifted me and carried me away. My arm felt prickly, like I'd been sleeping on it. Too groggy to wake up fully, I fell back into a deep sleep.

When I stumbled out of bed, nine hours later, my arm still felt tingly. I hadn't opened my eyes yet as I sat on the toilet and rested my head in my hands. What the—? My hand didn't feel like a hand. I raised my head and stared at my right arm. My breath caught in my throat. Sweat popped from my pores. In place of the arm I went to sleep with, there was a cast-like dark brown crust. I forced myself to resume breathing. In… out. In… out. The arm felt hot. I jumped off the toilet, shoved the deformity in the sink under cold water.

The crust splintered and fell away in one piece. Instead of fingers, my hand had become the head of an ant. The gold bracelets that had been on my wrist now hung from the ant's thorax, my arm from elbow to shoulder transformed into the abdomen. Legs and antennae unfolded and sprang out of what used to be my arm.

Dizzy and nauseated, I grabbed for the sink's edge with my left hand but missed. I collapsed. My head hit the floor, and everything went blank.

When I regained consciousness, I turned my head to the right. The sweetest bug eyes looked back at me, waiting, pleading. I knew what I had to do. I threw on clothes, rushed to my backyard, dropped to my knees and grabbed my garden trowel with my left hand. I dug deep into the loam where the peonies were blooming. My right arm instinctively dropped into the ground and within minutes was covered, becoming the queen ant of her own colony.

***

"So, Doctor, that's how my arm got like this."

I faced the doctor sitting on his wheelie stool. His eyes blinked rapidly, mouth slack, and he cocked his head. "Uh," he said. Very profound.

He took my arm in his hands and squeezed gently in a few places. "Any pain?"

"Nope. No pain. A little tender maybe."

"Any headaches?

"No headaches."

He scratched his forehead. "Hold on." He swiveled to open a supply drawer and withdrew a mirror. "Place your right arm in front of the mirror and tell me what you see in the reflection."

"Ah, look," I said. "Isn't she cute? A big beautiful giant ant has taken residence as my arm. I know I sound crazy, since I used to hate those little buggers. But my ants were Jesus Ants. They converted me. Now I see them as the lovable creatures they are." I hugged my ant arm.

"Interesting. Let me ask you, exactly how many poisonous chemicals would you say you've been exposed to over the years?"

I shook my head. "I don't understand the question."

"Never mind. May I take a photo of your arm? I want to call an associate who has more experience in this area." He snapped photos with his cell phone, "Wait right here."

He went in the hallway to make his call. The door didn't close all the way, so I heard him say, "Hey, Phil. Do you have a minute? I have a doozey of a case for you. This lady is the most delusional woman I've ever seen. She thinks her entire arm is an ant . . .Yep. One large arm-size arthropod ant."

Silence.

"I swear. I am not punking you . . . Serious as a hailstorm on a golf course. She believes it. . . Nope. No scratches on her arm. No fever, no headache. I'm texting you her pics for your files."

***

"So, Dr. Phil, that's how I ended up here with you."

Fern Goodman

Fern Goodman is a three-time FWA finalist and award-winning author and poet. Her short stories appear in four collection volumes and three other anthologies. She has published a book *Captured...the look of the dog* and a KDP short-read *Shooting up Hope*. Fern is also a SoulCollage® Facilitator, storyteller and comic.

ILLUSION

He speaks and they are mesmerized.
He weaves his spell and before their eyes
They see what he wants them to see.
His perfect words pulled from thin air
They hear them like almighty prayer.
They become what he wants them to be.

The time has come to ply his trade.
To execute this masquerade.
They are his, putty in his hands.
And there upon his ornate stage
He reveals a covered cage
To the believers, to his fans.

Then slowly with a raffish flair
He raises the cover in the air
Exposing the elephant in the room.
The crowds they gasp and cry with glee.
That can't believe what their eyes see.
Yes, he has them perfectly groomed.

He claps his hands. The cover drops.
The crowd's enthralled. Their talking stops.
He's set the perfect atmosphere.
He says some words as his hands hover.
Once again, he raises the cover.
The elephant has disappeared.

He gladly accepts their accolades
Although it's nothing but a charade.
For he is adept at delusion.
Was this poem about a magician
Or about a politician?
Think! Both can create an illusion.

Lee Fanning Hall

Lee is a published songwriter. Writing has always been integral to her life. Now retired, she devotes her time and talents to her two loves, poetry and music.

Break the Rules

Do not dare to use big words
Keep it simple, literate nerds
Be concise. Say what you mean but
don't embellish in between
Write to just an 8th grade level
So says our bourgeois regime.

The rule police have got us swindled
Corporate greed has made us kindled
Ordered schools of shrinking mindsets caring more of
tinks and gadgets, less of books while word sets dwindle
A plague of smaller syllables adheres to standards in the classes
Vocabulary scores are dropping as the futile flock amasses
Rue this day of lingual madness.

Gonomatopoeia are the days when words
could be a longish sound like what they meant
Reminiscent of a song
lasting only just so long.
Supercalifragilastics expialidociously
is stuck within a world of plastics
treading a precocious sea.
Illusive irony.
And so we drone in plainer terms
our notebook pages void with yearns for cleverness
Keys dancing through staccato tunes, clacking out our weary runes

But fiction dazzles.
It's an art that can't be tamed inside our hearts
The words flow freely spewing forth
vernacular regimes aside
creating rollercoaster rides while taking children
and adults to places where they never fly
Imagining perceptively what we all think and
what might be, tales unfolding from a page
while understanding grows by three

Squelch the words you find blasé
And make stuff up to find your way. Rescind,
tossing vanilla to the wind. Share your blood and
spill your tears. Do it loudly, thoughts gone wild
Find that feisty inner child and just let go
dive right in the very deep end of the page.
Escape the flow.

Perception's an illusive force
Dark hallways loom nearby hell's gate
Deep feelings slice out at the page but only when you
let them rage. Use that anger. Use the love
Embellish well, pontificate. Diversify and demonstrate you're not
afraid of when or how. Imperfect practice, use it now and
don't ask why.
Just let yourself syllabify.

Suzy Hart

Suzy Hart is an artist who thrives on creative endeavors and loves mind-boggling kinds of things, both archaic and new. She enjoys time in the sunshine with her husband and adventurous border collie, Cici.

THALIA'S PORTAL

She stood quietly by the waterfall which covered the mouth of a cave facing the river. It was the first night of the full moon, a time when magical things happened in this place. At midnight, the water pouring from the falls turned to liquid silver, and the cave behind it became a portal into a different realm. But only for the span of twelve heartbeats.

Thalia climbed the stair-step rocks at the side of the falls and slipped through the opening between the hillside and the cascading water, just as she had followed her mother's spirit many weeks earlier. Damp spray soaked her cape as she watched the water carefully, not certain how close it was to midnight. She peered behind her, into the depths of the cave, remembering the image of her mother vanishing into the darkness.

Glancing back at the falling torrent, she clutched a gourd dipper and watched the waterfall turn from clear to shimmering opaque. It was easy to count her thudding heartbeats, as she filled the gourd with splashes of silver. At the count of nine, she stepped deeper into the cave, one foot leaving the darkness and another foot stepping into daylight—emerging with her small treasure into another realm.

In the warm sunshine her mother, Adoni, greeted her with open arms. Thalia listened wide-eyed to her mother's instructions, as they walked among palm trees and orchids.

Together they delivered the solidified silver to a creature who worked with metals. Neither woman spoke to him, yet he understood he must fashion a medallion which would bestow power to this young maiden. Power beyond human strength or her mortal beauty. She would never have the brawn of a bear, but she would be able to turn any being into stone with a single look, so long as her hand touched the medallion.

On the day of Thalia's departure, Adoni placed the medallion on a leather cord and hung it around her daughter's neck. Thalia struggled to adjust the cord beneath the thick black tresses that fell to her waist. Her blue eyes sparkled with excitement, for she now had the power to overcome any adversaries. She would fulfill her destiny to protect her aging father, to take the place of the son he never had. And to provide him with a grandson to inherit and secure his great wealth.

Adoni raised a tent flap and motioned for Thalia to step inside . . . where she found herself back inside the cave with the smell of damp sand, the chirp of crickets, and the dream-like view from behind the waterfall.

***

After another day of overseeing her father's properties, Thalia rode her gray horse back to the riverbank with the enchanted waterfall. She longed for the cool refreshing air and the solitude. Her mind was in turmoil, thinking of numerous suitors who had asked for her hand in marriage. And her father had calmly refused each one, knowing she was devoted to him. She was his only child, his only heir. Any man she wed would control whatever she inherited from her father. In truth, any husband of hers might wish for, even hasten, her father's death. She would never consent to any such union.

While her horse drank deeply, she was startled by the sound of approaching hoofbeats. She watched as a man drew near on a black horse much larger than her own. His horse was so dark it shone with flashes of blue, like a raven's wing. It tossed its head imperiously, catching the scent of another horse. The man nodded his head to her in greeting, then directed his horse to the water.

The stranger was handsome, with copper colored hair, tanned skin, and liquid brown eyes. She had never found any man appealing. But this man looked like a god.

He acted as if he did not notice the plump breasts that bulged above her tight bodice, or the full lips, red as if stained from berries. His eyes seemed to flicker, however, when he caught sight of the medallion that hung below her neck.

"What brings such a fair lady into this wilderness, unescorted?" he asked.

Perhaps he *had* noticed. "This is my father's land; I need no escort here."

"Hmmm," he replied. "You are fortunate that I am not a ruthless oaf."

Thalia raised her head higher and stiffened her back. "I have no fear of you or any man."

The stranger approached her slowly, his horse snuffling and uneasy. He drew next to her, both horses disliking the close proximity, but steadied by their tightly-held reins. Her heart raced as his sizzling eyes connected with hers. "Aside from your haughty boldness," he said, "you might possibly make a good wife."

Thalia had decided this man was as perfect as she was likely to find. He could give her the kind of son she could be proud of. A fine grandson for her father.

"I have never been with a man," she said. "But you are comely and you look quite strong. Your eyes have intelligence. Perhaps I should mate with you."

The stranger looked like he had swallowed a lizard. "*Comely!* You think I am comely?"

"Perhaps striking is a better word." She was beginning to think this was too much trouble. Why would any man not be willing to immediately disrobe and accommodate her?

"When I am with a woman—of my choosing—it will be for the rest of my days."

"I only want your seed," she sputtered. "I do not want a husband!"

"And I do not want a trollop," he shouted, turning his horse away. He moved a short distance toward the forest, then turned back to face her, his eyes flashing.

Thalia suddenly hated this man she had offered herself to. She reached for her medallion, and touched only bare skin where it had been. Two horse-lengths away, the man reached inside his shirt and pulled out the silver disc, letting it dangle in the sunlight by its leather cord.

Enraged, she reached for the scabbard at her waist and pulled out a dagger. Just as she drew back to throw it, she felt it pulled away from her. It tumbled through the air, landing handle-first in the man's outstretched hand. With a smirk, he tossed the dagger and the medallion toward the riverbank, then . . .

***

A rapping sound startled her. Maybe her handmaid, knocking on her bedroom door?

"Babe, the pizza's here. You still writing?" Jimmy peered at her from the door he had cracked open.

Kate looked up from her laptop, fingers poised above the keys. She glanced around and took a deep breath. "Wow, I'm in another world! But I'm starving. Let me save this, and I'll take a break."

With a final click of the keys, she rose and stretched, started for the hallway. Her eyes were drawn back to the computer screen. Her own kind of portal, the other side of the waterfall. As always, the pull was strong.

Ellen Holder

Originally from North Carolina, Ellen is a happy resident of Central Florida. She and her husband are musical entertainers. She enjoys reading, gardening and dancing, but finds time for writing at all hours of the day or night.

THE PICNIC

Adrien always had a knack for picking the best spots. Even on this hot day, the huge pecan tree supplied ample shade. The breeze kicked up the blanket just as I was trying to pin it down with the basket on one end and our feet on the other. We both took off of our shoes using them as corner anchors. Mine were strappy white sandals. Adrien wore brown loafers with a tassel. Considerably larger than mine, he chuckled and relocated our shoes. One of his heavier shoes was now spooning my frilly sandal. He did the same at the other end.

"Aw, you're giving me goosebumps." I said.

He winked and blew me a kiss. "Did you remember my bubbly?"

Our picnic basket was overflowing. He always did say I over planned. "Of course." I pulled out a two liter Diet Coke. Twisting the cap, it suddenly burst open and began shooting out.

"Oh no!" I used my sweater to smother the eruption.

He laughed and pulled out two plastic champagne glasses. "Just like the real thing, eh?"

"Wait, it tastes better cold." I said. The wicker basket, now sticky with the spray of soda, had saved the contents from a soggy fate. Together we laid out our picnic buffet, consisting of two Monte Cristo club sandwiches, salt and vinegar chips for him, bar-b-que chips for me, grapes, watermelon, homemade potato salad, coleslaw, cake and most important, ice.

The cubes clinked and cracked as soon as they made contact with the hot soda. It was unseasonably warm for Spring so I put another handful in each flute, making the soda fizz once again.

"Are you happy?" I asked him.

"With you, always." He smiled, leaning over and giving me a kiss. I reveled in the scent of his cologne, his slight stubble tickling my chin.

Curiosity gnawed at me, "Is it good?"

He smacked his lips, then dabbed the corners of his mouth with a linen napkin, exaggerating the motion and pursing his lips. "Best sandwich ever."

I bumped my foot against his. "You know very well I'm not asking about the sandwich."

He took another bite and waved the napkin dismissively. Making unwavering eye contact, he chewed as slow as possible, drawing me into a frustrating staring eye contest for which I blinked over twenty times by the time he finished his bite.

"I win." He smiled.

"Really, tell me the truth." I insisted.

He handed me the bag of bar-b-que chips, and then held my hands when I reached for them. "Everything is fine." He kissed the top of my right hand. "You worry too much."

The gesture made my heart swell. He'd done it on our first date and every date ever since. Even before he knew I was a sucker for old movies and gallantry. I sat back munching on the chips while he piled on a generous serving of each of the side items on his paper plate. He looked fantastic. Tanned, trim with just enough muscle to make me swoon. His hair was blond again, the way it always got when he was out in the sun. Handsome and a fast eater, it took him only a few minutes to clean off his plate and get second helpings, which he consumed just as quickly.

"Are you ready for dessert?" I asked.

He had firm, muscular abs under his shirt, but he rubbed his belly pushing it out, "Maybe in a few minutes."

I fished out two books from the basket and we laid back and read. The filtered sunlight danced on the pages when the wind ruffled the leaves. I didn't notice when I fell asleep, but I felt his love nestled against me, like our two spooning shoes.

We'd been married thirty years. An eternity for some. Not nearly enough for me. He'd always been athletic. I considered yoga exercise enough. We were a perfect match of strength and flexibility. We'd raised three wonderful kids. The year our youngest started college we took four vacations to the places we'd always dreamed of, a castle on the Swiss Alps, snorkeling in New Zealand, an overwater bungalow in Bora Bora and an excursion to Alaska.

Alaska had been my idea. In hindsight, dealing with extreme cold was not my forte. Adrien had attempted to persuade me to another more tropical location. But seeing the whales and glaciers had made it worth the subzero temperatures. He'd been glued to me those weeks. Always considerate, he was ready with hot chocolate and his loving arms to warm me up. At times I felt we'd come back fused together. My shivering body didn't give him a moment's rest until our flight dropped us off back onto warm Texas soil.

That's what my picnic reminded me of. The way he had spooned me while we slept, keeping me warm throughout the cold Alaskan cruise ship nights. I stretched my toes and sat up. Thirsty, I took a sip of my champagne soda only to scrunch my nose at the watered down taste. The ants must have taken a nap with me because none of them had raided our food, which was incredibly lucky since we hadn't eaten our dessert yet. After gathering up the leftovers, I took the cake out of the white, cardboard pastry box.

"Don't look. I want it to be a surprise."

Adrien continued to lay on his side and pretended to snore. I placed the napkin over his eyes, just in case, while I lit the candle.

"Ta-Da!" I said letting him see again. "Your favorite, double fudge cake with chocolate filing, chocolate icing, chocolate shavings, chocolate sprinkles and strawberries."

I sang to him and he blew out the candle.

"What did you wish for?"

He held one finger over his lips and shook his head.

"I know what I'd wish for." I said. Retrieving two forks, we didn't even bother with the plates as we scooped up decadent bites. When we finished, I took the last item out of the basket, set it to one side and began collecting all our belongings. When everything was tucked back into the overflowing wicker basket, I slipped on my shoes and folded up the blanket.

The last item was a bouquet of brightly colored flowers, something which he'd always brought me. "I never thought to ask you what your favorite flower was," I said, a single tear running down my cheek. Quickly brushing it away, I retrieved another candle and lit it. The warm wax began to dribble onto my fingers, but I ignored it, not wanting to feel anything but him.

Closing my eyes, I whispered, "I'd wish for a million more days with you." Then I blew out the candle as the wind wisped my hair. After a few moments I reopened them and slipped the flowers into the marble vase. I adjusted the green satin ribbon. It was his favorite color.

I gathered up the basket, draped the blanket over my arm and looked back one more time. Adrien Link, Beloved husband and father, 1964-2019.

"Happy Birthday, my sweet."

Laura Holian

A Texas A&M University graduate, Laura unwinds by relishing in Florida's lovely landscape on her cruiser bike and feeling the water lap at her toes during walks along the beach. Her perfect day off would include a movie, some time to read or draw, and chocolate cake.

The Visit

I stood in the sanitized hallway of Saint Anthony's Children Hospital just outside the cancer ward, my head throbbed, and my body trembled at the thought: facing those children would crumble me. At forty-two, I was decades older than the kids behind those white double doors. Yet, the power of their innocent faces was too much for me. I couldn't believe I let my agent talk me into this with a cheap bottle of Merlot.

I spun, poised to leave, when Jeannie, the perky nurse who coordinated this visit, appeared out of nowhere. "Ms. Springfield! Thank you for coming. The kids barely slept a wink last night."

"Um, yeah." I fidgeted.

She urged me forward with a hand on my back. "Come."

We emerged through the doors into a long, stanch room. The sun shone brightly from windows at the far end. A blunt table near the doors were cluttered in coloring pages and crayons. A half-dozen beds lined each side of the room, each with a child perched and hugging one of my Dragon Lure books. Some had Book One, others Book Two or Three. Their lively eyes and shiny scalps made them look like life-sized, hairless baby dolls.

I crept forward behind Jeannie's springy trot.

"Look who arrived, boys and girls. Your favorite author, Ms. Sandra Springfield."

The kids bounced and clapped.

"They're all yours, Ms. Springfield." Jeannie ducked to the side, leaving me alone to face the troops.

My throat tightened. "Uh, hello. I—" Cold flushed over me. I locked eyes with the little boy at the end. His floppy hair, bright green eyes, squeezable rounded cheeks. For a second, I swore it was Charlie, my boy. "Um…I…"

"Why don't you tell them," Jeannie jumped in, "how you thought of your exciting book series?"

"Well…" I began, my mind scrambling like confused ants. I swallowed.

"Yes, um. You see my son, Charlie. He loved dragons. We'd go the library, and that's all he wanted to read. And he knew them all. Hydra. The Amphithere. The Wyvern. The Lindworm. He'd pin his drawings on every wall."

A little girl bounced and held out a drawing. "Look at my dragon!"

"And mine!"

"Yes, yes. They're very nice."

I blinked and saw Charlie lying on his belly at the center of his bedroom. Crayons and paper spread everywhere. He looked up and smiled. "Check out my Wyvern, Mommy!"

"Lovely." I knelt next to him, rubbing his back and bald head.

"He's scary but gentle. The only dragon who can dislodge emeralds with his diamond tail without damaging the jewel's magic."

"That so?" I was the fantasy writer, but Charlie always knew more than me. I caressed his smooth head, a reminder of the pain he suffered with every dose of chemo. Over time I watched him grow thinner, weaker, my beautiful flower wilting in the harsh sunlight.

I blinked. I was back in the cancer ward, a dozen kids smiling, shifting on their beds. My stomach twisted, knowing the pain they've suffered, the weathering path they were on.

A hand shot up.

"Um… yes?"

"When's the fourth book coming out?"

"Well, I'm not done writing it."

"When will you be done?"

"Um… I don't know." I hadn't written a word in three years. After Charlie died, I sat in his bedroom, the bed unmade, hand-drawn dragons everywhere, Crayons scattered. The quiet house stripped away every word, syllable, and story from my soul.

The dozen kids stared, their faces hungry for the unwritten book that lay sleeping in my abandoned imaginary world.

"It takes," I started, "a long time to write a book."

A little girl raised a hand. "Will you finish in a month?"

"Uh…"

"Because," she continued, "my last round of chemo is this month. And my doctor said…" She looked down. "There won't be another." By the time she lifted her head, tears glistened.

A tide swept over the kids. Their smiles, their bounce, their excitement—gone.

I felt their loss, their pain and helplessness, mirrored in Charlie's eyes that grew foggy and distant in his last days. I was too late, for Charlie and these kids. By the time I complete the book, sell it to the publisher, and get it in print, some of these kids may be—gone.

Silence pervaded the room. Even Jeannie, still in the corner, said nothing, though her face pleaded. Seconds ticked, tears filled little eyes.

Suddenly, something inside me snapped. I leapt forward. My shoes slapped the tiled floor. "Listen!"

The kids gasped.

I said, "Everyone, close your eyes. Close them."

One-by-one, every pair of eyes shut.

"Now, picture in your mind, a cave."

A kid opened his eyes. "A cave?"

"Eyes closed!"

He shut them.

"A dark cave, giant stalactites dangling from above. A fog rolls in, surrounding you on all sides, and with it comes a foreign scent. You hear a sound, deep, menacing. You spin. A giant figure stands before you, three stories high. With an orange glow cutting through its sharp teeth, you know this giant Amphithere Dragon. Purple. Wings tipped with red claws."

"Draconia!" a girl called.

"Yes. Our beloved Draconia. She steps forward. You're afraid at first. But there's a pained look in her eyes. Someone has left her. Someone has broken her heart. Without words, with a mere weary droop of her blue eyes, you know, you can hear in your mind a cry for help. A cry to help her… find the love who… has left her."

The boy from the back asked, "Is this the next book?"

"Yes." I smiled. "And you're going to write it."

The kids reopened their eyes with smiles and mouths hung open.

"Us?" a girl asked.

"Yes! Each one of you pictured yourselves in the cave, alone with Draconia. She needs your help to rescue her loved one, to combat the evil forces of the Lindworms. To outrun the dragon hunters in every realm."

"When do we—"

"Now." I dashed for the stack of paper sitting on a small table near the room's entrance. "Here. Take some paper. Grab a crayon. Draw. Write. Continue this adventure before it's too late, for Draconia's sake… and your own."

The children sprang from their beds. They grabbed a couple pages and returned to their beds. They laughed and smiled and shared ideas and stories and scenes and heroes and villains.

I encouraged each kid as I skirted from bed to bed. After several minutes, I sank toward the doors. Jeannie touched my arm. I turned.

Her eyes glassed. "You truly brought joy to these kids." She breathed. "You don't know how… how much they needed this." She faced the kids. "How much they needed an escape from, you know."

I nodded and glanced at the kids. I knew their stories were illusions, fantasies, distractions from real life. Their treatments would continue. Their conditions may worsen. Yet, I sensed a truth I had somehow forgotten. "These illusions have the power of healing." I pushed at the door.

"You leaving now?"

I nodded. "It's time for me to write." I patted her arm, smiled warmly at the children, and walked down the hospital corridor, now with a lighter heart.

John Hope

John Hope is an award-winning short story, speculative fiction, historical, and young adult fiction writer. His work appears in various anthologies, in print, audiobooks, and adapted into plays. Mr. Hope, a native Floridian, loves to travel with his wife and two kids and enjoys running. Read more at: www.johnhopewriting.com.

DERAILED

Kayla stared as the words, *talk to me*, faded from her phone's screen. She wove her thick, honey-blond hair into a long braid, grabbed her backpack, and left the bedroom.

"'Morning, pretty girl." Aunt Tiffany fried eggs on the stove while the twins ate their breakfast in matching highchairs.

"Play, KayKay," shrieked Norah.

"Me. Me." Hannah banged on her tray.

Kayla kissed the two blond heads. At eighteen months, the toddlers were into everything. "Later. KayKay has school."

Aunt Tiffany spun around. "Could you keep an eye on the Destructive Duo? I have to call the art gallery about my showing." She disappeared into the living room.

"I'll miss the bus." No answer. Kayla shrugged and handed each girl a sippy cup. She didn't care about school, but one more tardy meant detention. Her aunt never understood high school start times.

Aunt Tiffany's voice seeped into the kitchen. "Yeah, Kayla can watch the kids if you need me this afternoon."

Kayla sighed and opened her geometry book.

"No, she's fine. Poor Lindsay and Dave died six months ago, but Kayla's handling it. She's amazing, and the twins adore her."

Kayla's stomach dropped. The page blurred as a tear splashed over a list of theorems.

"Dave worked for the railroads and Lindsay cleaned houses. They never had two dimes to rub together."

Kayla closed her eyes and listened for the train whistles that always filled her old row house. She loved the mournful wail as it seeped into her dreams and greeted her in the early morning. But at her aunt's, all Kayla heard was toddler babble.

"Honey!" Aunt Tiffany's voice made her jump. "You'll miss the bus."

"Right. Bye!" Kayla shoved the book into the pack.

Aunt Tiffany handed her a lunch. "This evening, we'll look at colors and talk about decorating your bedroom."

"Sure, Aunty." Kayla rushed out the back door, the soft strains of "Have a good day," following behind.

Kayla walked down the street. Same houses, same cars, same trees, same bushes. How could anything this expensive look so monotonous?

She was a half-block away when she saw the school bus speed off. Kayla groaned. Returning home meant waiting for her aunt. She'd miss math class for sure. Luckily the school was only two miles away, and it was one of those rare, balmy March days when the sky was blue and the air almost warm. She might as well walk. A quarter-mile later, Kayla stopped. Her aunt thought she caught the bus. The school probably thought she was sick. There were no girlfriends and certainly no boyfriends who'd miss her. The thought hurt, but it meant she was free.

Kayla turned around. At first, she wasn't aware she walked in any specific direction. It took her awhile to figure out she was heading towards the train tracks. Just outside of town, the rails went over Stonybrook Creek and disappeared into a hill. When she was younger, a gang from her old neighborhood used to climb above the tunnel and perch on the boulders. They'd watch the trains fade into the blackness and dare each other to follow the cars into the dark passage. Kayla exhaled as if punched in the gut. She always had trouble making friends, but at least the kids in the old neighborhood hung out with her.

As the sun rose higher, Kayla reached the creek, climbed up, and sat on the main rock above the tunnel entrance. The light felt good on her face. She leaned back and let her thoughts wander. The last fight with her dad. The shopping trip she and Mom never made it to. Each "I love you" and apology that would now never be said. All gone, vanished in an instant, lost forever.

Kayla struggled to breathe. It felt as if a hand crushed her heart.

***

The phone's alarm chimed. Kayla fished it out of her pocket and looked down.

Silvergirl: can u talk

Kayla's fingers flew across the keyboard.

Darkmatter: I shattered. Millions of pieces. Never come together again. Can't think. Pissed off at everything. Why did they die? Why am I still here?

Kayla came across the suicide chatroom a month ago. She'd never texted much before and got teased for writing in complete sentences. But for once there were others like her. It's where she met Silvergirl.

Silvergirl: u can't give up.

Darkmatter: I lost my family, my friends. I'm a loser. I can't sleep, no one at this new school knows me or likes me. I'll never have good friends again. I'm too quiet. Too boring.

Silvergirl: ur depressed. depression is the big liar. u feel alone, helpless, hopeless. ur not.

Darkmatter: I don't want this shitty life.

A whistle blew. Kayla glanced at her watch. It was the eastbound train. *Mom, if I show up, will you be mad at me?* She didn't know what to expect after death, but anything was better than this emptiness.

Silvergirl: u can't control life. only how you deal with it. im your friend. i understand.

Darkmatter: How could you?

Silvergirl: my sister took her life. i couldn't stop her.

Darkmatter: So you're making yourself feel better by trying to save me?

Silvergirl: this is about u. not me. don't want to lose u 2.

Darkmatter: You're not here. My aunt and uncle don't know me at all. As long as I keep smiling, they think I'm okay.

Silvergirl: so stop smiling. talk 2 them

Darkmatter: I hear the train. I can catch this one. I just have to jump.

Silvergirl: go home. talk 2 ur aunt. from what u said she loves u.

A cold wind blew across Kayla's body, ruffling her hair and causing her to shiver.

Darkmatter: I'm so tired. I just want everything to be over. Thanks for listening to me and being my only friend.

Silvergirl: don't do it. hopelessness, aloneness is an illusion. ur not alone. ur not hopeless. darkmatter ru there? ur parents wouldn't want this for u. talk to ur aunt.

Kayla's finger hovered over the off button. She closed her eyes, drew in deep breaths, then looked at the phone. Silvergirl still texted.

The whistle blew again, closer now. Kayla and her mom used to sit on the tracks to feel the vibrations of the oncoming cars. The memory made her smile. The engine rounded the curve and sped toward her, dragging a line of boxcars and flatbeds. Kayla looked at the phone screen.

Silvergirl: do u really want to die? theres always hope.

With a whoosh, the train entered the tunnel.

Kayla stood up. Do I want this? She inched closer to the edge, railcars still rumbling below her. She hesitated. There's always hope? Maybe. One thing for sure—her parents would kill her if they knew what she was doing. The irony of that last thought made Kayla step back with a laugh that sounded more like a sob.

Silvergirl: darkmatter? ru there?

Kayla dragged in a ragged breath and wondered what she would say to Aunt Tiffany. Her fingers stabbed at the screen.

Darkmatter: Missed the train.

She picked up her backpack and began the downward climb.

Sharon Keller Johnson

Sharon moved to Florida over thirty years ago and raised a family, taught school and tried to stay sane—unsuccessfully. Now she writes, paints and tutors math.

No Good Deed...

Despite sunrise still being thirty minutes away, most of the cul-de-sac residents stood two-deep outside Judge Robinson's house. The yellow crime-scene tape held them at a respectful distance.

Pulsing red and blue lights from half a dozen emergency vehicles made the cul-de-sac's home facades and wet pavement resemble a disco dance floor, but no one danced.

A member of the crowd speculated, "I bet that fat-ass judge had a heart attack."

Andrew Sinclair didn't respond, but he was pretty sure it wasn't a heart attack or stroke or fall, as others had offered. Andrew endured the early morning bone-penetrating cold and rain for one reason: verification that his aim had been true. He knocked rain off the bill of his baseball cap and pulled up his jacket zipper as far as possible. A shiver welled up in him.

The mansion's front door opened.

Andrew's mood morphed to the giddiness of a kid at Christmas.

A few seconds later the ambulance crew exited and wheeled an empty gurney to its truck.

Andrew had to bite his tongue to prevent a yelp of glee, but a tear of joy mixed with rain on his cheek.

A local cop in a yellow slicker took down the crime-scene tape and allowed the ambulance to drive through, wipers playing a steady beat. No more than a minute later a white van with Coroner stenciled on the driver's door crested the hill. It was all Andrew needed to see. He turned, strolled down the hill, and stopped next to his car. The cold no longer bothered him. When the white van passed, he snapped off a left-handed salute with his middle finger extended. He smiled.

One down, one to go.

***

Andrew relaxed in the warmth of his trailer the remainder of the morning. At noon he checked the local news shows. They all played the same grainy black-and-white footage from a doorbell camera. In it a burly man lifted a rifle, fired a single shot, and then disappeared into the barren brush and trees across the street. The crawl across the bottom of the screen asked residents to be on the lookout for a Hispanic or African-American male between five ten and six feet, two hundred to two hundred twenty pounds.

Andrew smiled.

His plan to wait for a rainy day seemed to have paid off. The rain reduced the chance of someone being out for a walk. It also made cameras much less effective at recording clear pictures. He had worn an umpire's chest protector under a sweatshirt, hood up, and a dark padded jacket to make himself appear heavier than his 165 pounds. He added thick-soled boots to provide the appearance of being taller than five feet seven inches. He even applied makeup to darken his skin. He needed to be something that would appear to be there, but when people tried to put a name to it, they wouldn't be able to. So far, so good.

Shortly after six that evening, he began preparations for his final act of revenge.

***

The damp dreariness had carried into the evening. Bar patrons hurried to their cars, heads down, stepping over puddles in the poorly lit parking lot behind Casey's Bar and Grill.

Andrew glanced at his watch; seven o'clock. She'd be out soon.

He sat in his car, rifle at the ready, the same rifle that killed Judge Robinson twelve hours earlier.

Sure enough, at 7:07 Assistant District Attorney Deborah Ann Coltin, the curvy blonde, exited Casey's. With the short choppy steps of someone wearing spike heels and a too-tight skirt, she worked her way across the parking lot avoiding puddles as if they represented everything evil. She held the designer handbag over her head as a makeshift umbrella.

He clicked the safety off.

She pressed a key fob, and lights went on in a white Lexus.

His cheek nestled the rifle stock.

She did a sidestep dance between a BMW and her Lexus

The scope crosshairs found her face.

She opened the door.

He held his breath and squeezed the trigger.

***

Andrew strode down the line of tombstones, head up, shoulders back, smile on his face. "Damn, I'm good. Pa would be proud."

The media had played the two killings up big, but the authorities had only grainy footage from a doorbell camera and a fuzzy security camera video from Casey's. It showed a dark sedan, no license plate, no lights on, driving down the street. The driver's left arm extended out the window with the middle finger raised.

His planning had paid off. He was nothing but an apparition, an illusion to the police. They had no clues and no evidence, nor would they ever. Within thirty minutes of Deborah Ann's demise, the dark sedan was in a chop shop being disassembled. The rifle had been melted down.

Mission accomplished.

Andrew stopped in front of a short gray tombstone that he knew well. The chiseled name stated Robert A. Sinclair. The inscription read "Son and brother. Gone but not forgotten."

He made the sign of the cross, knelt on one knee, and asked God to watch over his little brother. He crossed himself once again and rose.

"Well, Bobby, I did it. I killed those two assholes who put you in prison." He fist-bumped the headstone. "But I guess you know that, seeing how you're probably already in heaven. I got even for you, bro. They ain't never gonna railroad an innocent man again. I know they wasn't the one what shanked you, but they put you there. They was wrong, and now they know it." He wiped a tear from an eye. "You can rest in peace now."

He brushed away a twig that leaned against his brother's headstone.

"Next time I visit I'll bring some grass seed to fill these bare spots. You'll have a thick green carpet to keep you warm."

Off to the right a backhoe lumbered down the row of headstones toward him. He stepped aside to let it pass, but the noisy machine stopped short of Bobby's grave. Its driver turned off the ignition, and a large black cloud escaped the smokestack. He stepped down and approached. "Sorry to interrupt your peace and quiet, but I need to dig a new hole." The man motioned to the empty plot next to Bobby's grave.

"No problem. I hope they lived a long life, not like my brother." The last couple of words caught in his throat.

The worker wagged his head. "This is where Judge Robinson's going."

Andrew's stomach spasmed. "Here? Next to my brother?"

"Yes, sir, tomorrow." He returned to his machine and restarted it.

Andrew dropped to a knee and placed his hand on Bobby's marker. "I don't know what to say. I can't believe it." He pounded the top of the tombstone. "I thought I done good for you. Now one of the assholes is going right next to you." He pounded the top of the tombstone again. "I planned it all out. I thought you and Pa would be proud of me. I guess Pa was right again. No good deed goes unpunished."

Henry James Kaye

Born and raised in Pittsburgh, Henry had successful careers in banking, entrepreneurship, technology and real estate. His passion, writing, produced multiple Collections stories, several published books, and two RPLA winners. He married Nancy over 40 years ago, they have 3 children and one grandchild. He lives in Longwood, Florida.

Good Morning, George

Ones keep the fireplace warm. Fives pave through our lawn. Tens are insulation that uproot framed pictures and cascade down the wall like wild vines taking over. We have so much money, we've run out of places to put it. The house glows in a mixture of silver and gold.

My husband swirls a tightly wound hundred in his coffee, mixing cream and sugar.

"What are your plans for today, dear?" I bring a glass of iced lemonade to my lips.

He gazes through the large picture window in our living room, observes the ripples of yellow, orange, and crimson splashing across the sky from the sunrise. He breathes deeply and relaxes into the smell of the fresh apple crisp I took out of the oven five minutes ago. "I'm thinking a walk through the park." He picks up the newspaper, adjusting his Rose-Colored Glasses.

"The park sounds nice, dear." I reach for his hand and lace our fingers.

He looks as handsome as the day we first met. A strong, square jaw, well-trimmed black hair, and there wasn't a single gray mixed in. He doesn't look a day over twenty-five, a feat after thirty years of marriage.

A breeze blows through the hallway and wraps around the dining room. My arms become dotted in goosebumps. Turns out money makes for poor insulation, but at least the house is everything else we've ever wanted.

"Do you want me to turn the heat up?" he says.

"Don't worry. We'll eat, then go for a walk. That'll warm us up." Standing up, the Audio Aids come loose and spill out of my ears. My husband's voice cracks like static, a radio station breaking up. I press the small plugs back until they're secure, and my husband's voice is clear again. "Did you say something, dear?"

"No, honey," he says.

I slip into the kitchen to grab a pair of plates, utensils, and a knife. "Do you need more coffee?"

"I won't say no." He chuckles.

I place the plates on the table and make another trip to the kitchen to retrieve the coffee pot. Returning to the table, I empty the pitcher into his cup a little too long, the cup overflows, but the table cloth doesn't dampen.

"Thank you, dear."

I put the pitcher on the table and pick up the knife. I take hold of the crisp tin and press the knife into the flaky crust. The fruity filling is too dense to cut. Perhaps my blade is dull and needs to be sharpened again. I grit my teeth and press it down. A bit of pink juice squirts out.

"It smells delicious." He turns the newspaper page.

"Any new developments?" I ask. A piece of the crisp comes free. I grab a fork and slip its edge underneath the triangle I'd cut. As I remove it from the tin, pinkish and yellow juice drip from the mixed fillings and gather in a puddle at the bottom of the tin. I set the slice down and slide the plate across the table.

"Governor says the war's over. Economy's about to boom."

"What are we gonna do with *more* money?" I point around the room with the knife, laughing.

"Honestly, I think he's talking out his ass." He exchanges the newspaper for his fork.

I start to cut my piece out of the pan, but catch my finger on the knife's edge. I yelp and jump back. I drop the knife to the floor. My glasses fly off my face and I slap my hand over my eyes. "Oh dear--where--honey, do you see my glasses anywhere?" I cover my eyes with my hand as I lower to the floor.

"I don't see anything, honey. Sorry."

I grope the floor and yell, pricking myself with the knife. My eyes open and I look at my hand. A red line brightens across my dirty, gray index finger.

"Honey, are you okay?"

"Yeah, I just had an accident." I look to him, but instantly cover my mouth to hold back the scream and vomit I feel coming. His skin is pale, cold, and rotting off the bone. Maggots have bore a hole in his cheek. His skin and the chair are connected in some places. His hip bones are exposed where he has no skin anymore His mouth hangs open, teeth pile in his lap, mostly yellowed, some brown, and his eye sockets are empty, surrounded by black, red, and green rot.

"Honey, you don't look well. Maybe you should lay down," he says, but his body doesn't move.

"No! I have to find my glasses first." I spot them across the rotting wood floor. I crawl to them and slip them back on, but cracks in the glass splintered my vision. In some fragments, I see my home as it should be mixed with the nightmare I don't want to see: water-logged and fungus-plagued wood infect our expensive marble floors. The large, living room picture window is shattered and shows a mixture of the most beautiful sunrise I've ever seen and a thick, gray, cloud, the remnants of the last nuclear bomb that dropped. Then my beautiful husband who wasn't himself.

"Trade me glasses, dear. Mine are broken."

"Please, take them." In a quarter of my lenses, he extends the glasses to me. In the broken fragments, his arms hang at his sides and his expression is empty. I close my eyes and replace my glasses with his before slipping the broken ones onto him. Once they're on his face, they look perfect, not even a small scratch. I stroke his cheek with the back of my hand. "You look perfect."

"You too, honey."

"Everything's perfect." I lean in and kiss his forehead. I finish cutting out my piece of apple crisp and sit down with my husband. We eat breakfast together and, just as we said, we go for a perfect walk in the most perfect weather I can imagine.

Ian Kirkpatrick

Ian moved to Florida from the frozen tundra of Alaska. She hopes her stories not only transport the reader to another place, but might make them tilt their heads to the side. We live in a strange place and humans are strange creatures. The absurdity is endless.

MEMORIES

AH! Those memories of days that have long ago past,
threaten to vanish and say, "we won't last."
How aging and time can dull all the senses,
and make it so hard and put up such tall fences.
They vanish like ghosts in a flame on the hearth,
only to spark again, given a start.

The more time that passes, it's harder to see.
Is that face in the mirror a really worn me?
Like a cauldron that's nestled on top of a fire,
those memories need stirring a constant reminder!

Memories of those that have gone long before,
linger like sweet scents that pass through the door.
I speak to them constantly, sharing a thought,
as they tell me again if I should or should not.
I hear them, I see them, their talents - their flaws,
that help keep me grounded and then give me pause.

Now it's your turn to seize them and put them in place,
and to match every story to each person's face.
Think where you came from, remember your roots,
and the people who sowed them - their values - their truths.
All they were part of is part of you now,
then flows to your offspring and spreads like a plow
over fields of new memories now theirs to recall,
and pass on to their kin who'll remember us all.

Catch them, those memories, they're fading and dim.
Take time to remember that Her or that Him.
A picture, a story, can trigger that start,
and force you to wander through tales of the heart.

The good and the bad, oh those visions aren't fair.
They bring up the sadness then drop you off there,
to be changed in an instant to days in the sun
and places of pleasure - of music - of fun!

That's the key to these memories, you must take them all.
You can't change an action nor sidestep a fall.
It is what it is and you're better off for it.
Take what it's left you, and move on and store it.

So venture on forward to life's next best thrill
and keep making those footprints that others will fill,
but keep stirring that cauldron that keeps us alive
where we live in your memory and continue to thrive!

Alice Klaxton

Alice grew up in New Hampshire, and moved to Florida in 2009 to enjoy her retirement.

Inner Beauty and All that Jazz

The cliché that God gave me the face
that I deserve seems somewhat reasonable
if I accept wrinkles, sags, and lines as proof
of some mischievous divine intervention.
The first time I looked into the mirror
and beheld the force of gravity dragging
my chin to my toes, the heavens trembled,
sending once-taut skin south of the border,
like a deflated balloon screaming for air.
My mother's words were illusory at best:
"Only inner beauty matters in the end."
In a world cruelly obsessed with youth,
those who view aging as a nasty blight
do not acknowledge that I have evolved
from a chrysalis to a mature woman.

I remember the illusion of my youth,
that desire to shed my juvenile face
and suddenly become someone glamorous—
an incandescent jewel of a woman, secure
in her attractiveness, radiant with hope.
No longer is my skin dew-kissed and firm,
my features clearly defined and chiseled,
but my mother was correct—my beauty
lies within—awaiting excavation, a discovery
to be made by those who seek hidden riches
that have been carefully guarded through years
of protecting the vulnerability of my soul.

Linda Kraus

Linda Kraus has taught university courses in literature and film studies. She has published poetry in several literary journals and anthologies and is currently editing two collections of poetry.

The Camping Trip

Sandra rubbed her eyes certain what she was seeing was a mirage. It could be. She hadn't had coffee in four days. The swill Patrick passed off could stand up and greet you. Her taste buds officially went on strike after the first sip. Despite the caffeine withdrawal, they still refused to compromise. Not that she blamed them.

She required more than the powder non-dairy creamer Patrick offered. At the very least he could have gotten her some single serve flavored creamers, a nice hazelnut or pumpkin spice. They didn't require refrigeration and she'd still feel civilized. She'd even settle for vanilla. Though what she really hankered for was a raspberry latte from Starbucks. She also required a bathroom, which was how she had stumbled into this part of the woods. So much for the camping experience.

She shook the thoughts of coffee away and stepped out from behind her chosen bush. A downed branch cracked; the bushes ahead rustled as whatever had passed her moved deeper into the woods. Sandra, not exactly of sound mind, followed. She hadn't gone far when she stumbled into a protected glade and there in the middle, was the creature. Her heart fluttered then sank.

It was just a horse. Well cared for, she could see that, its large white hindquarters looked like they had been brushed until they glowed. The glossy white tail swished back and forth, as it slowly shifted its weight from one hoof to another. The head never lifting from the ground it grazed. Did people ride here? Patrick had been so excited about the trip, prattling on about untouched forests and the pristine lake that she might have missed a few facts.

"Hey horsey." She held out her hand as if offering a treat. Oblivious to her the animal tore at the grass. "Here horsey, horsey." It shifted again. The tail flicked, making a loud whack against its right flank. Annoyance she assumed at the gargantuan mosquitoes she too, smacked away.

There was no way this horse was wild. It would have run off the moment it sensed her presence. So, what was it doing alone this deep in the woods? Could it have thrown its rider? Sandra backed up, circled to her left, looking for some sign of humanity. "Hello." She called. "I found your horse."

She walked along the outer edges of the glade; peering back into the woods as she searched certain there had to be a trail or campsite nearby. Meanwhile the horse kept grazing. She was parallel to it now. There were no loose reins or a lead line trailing it in the grass. Maybe it belonged to the park ranger. Patrick would know.

Then her eyes caught it, the horn sticking out from the middle of its head. Had to be a joke, unicorns weren't real. Except the creature looked just as magical as it had earlier, wasn't that why she had followed it? Why her heart now raced even as she said, "Nah can't be." She scanned the nearby trees for cameras. "Good one, Patrick, real funny."

At the sound of her voice, the unicorn raised its head and looked her square in the face. The horn didn't wobble. The twisted spire looked, actually, quite sharp. It snorted, stretched out its thick neck and sniffed the air. God, it was everything a unicorn should be. The most beautiful brown eyes, expressive and round, highlighted by thick lashes gazed into her very soul. Every girly childhood dream blossomed and she squealed in soft delight. So what if it was a hoax. She had never seen a more majestic horse with its soft white muzzle and flared pink nostrils.

Not wanting to spook it, Sandra hastily backed out of the clearing and ran off in the direction she had come. "Patrick! Patrick! Come quick!"

She heard a clatter of noise, like a pot overturning, then the stomp of her boyfriend's feet through the underbrush. "What? What is it?" His face was ashen and filled with fright, "You okay?" Sandra nodded. Her breath suddenly failed. She wanted to scream, cry and laugh all at the same time. "Whatever it was, you scared it worse than it scared you."

She shook her head, grabbed at the air, gobbling it down as if she'd been deprived. "You'll never believe," She chewed her lip, motioned with jerked fingers for him to hurry. "Quick." She scampered towards him and then away. "Before it's gone."

Impatient, Sandra grabbed his hand, pulling Patrick off his feet. "Whoa. What's gotten into you?"

"You'll see." She wasn't even sure she could find the clearing. All the bushes looked the same but then Sandra spotted the dropped roll of toilet paper and slowed. "Through here."

They retraced her path to the clearing and just when she thought it really had been a mirage, Sandra saw it. The unicorn had migrated towards the far end of the glade and now stood sheltered beneath an ancient oak. Dappled sunlight glinted off its coat through the branches. Sandra crouched down and pointed, "There. See it?"

"Is that," Patrick paused, "a horse?"

"Unicorn." Sandra said. Her voice softened, "Isn't it beautiful?"

Clearly amused he grinned, "You saw a horn?"

"I'm not crazy."

"Certainly not, just caffeine deprived." He passed her and headed out into the open.

"Patrick," her stomach knotted, "don't."

"I'll be fine." He smiled, winking as if this were all an elaborate ruse; she relaxed thinking maybe it was. He had said he had a surprise for her. What if this was some fairytale themed proposal? Be just like him to woo her with a plastic horn taped on top of a horse's head.

She watched him approach the animal, clicking his tongue and murmuring soft words of reassurance. One second the unicorn was grazing, the next all four hooves shot out. It bolted across the clearing.

Turning, it charged towards Patrick in a thunderous frenzy. Ears back, head lowered. The point of the unicorn's horn cut through the grass with the precision of a shark's dorsal fin. Patrick didn't move. "Killer unicorn coming my way," he said, laughing.

Then the unthinkable happened. The beast raised its head, the horn aimed chest high.

"Holy Mother . . ." The rest died in her throat. She squeezed her eyes shut but heard Patrick scream until with a bone crunching thud he stopped. "Patrick?" Sandra scrambled forward. Tears blocked her vision. With a shaky hand she wiped them away. He was sprawled ten feet from the beast, bleeding but alive. "Patrick!"

She tried not to stare but was transfixed by the now bloodstained horn. The unicorn reared. Pawing the air as it screeched in some dark, horrific octave no animal should make.

Two foals raced from the cover of the ancient oak tree and descended upon Patrick. Beautiful and otherworldly, they looked so sweet nuzzling Patrick. Weakly he called out, "Run, Sand-"

The foals lifted their heads, muzzles covered in gore. Patrick was silent. Sandra blinked. Was any of this real? Screaming she tore off through the trees, running blind. From behind her, the sound of hooves neared."

Teresa Little

Teresa Little writes short stories, and poetry. Her writing interests range from Mainstream Literary to Fantasy. She is currently working on her debut novel.

JEALOUSY

The door squealed as Sebastian, using his shoulder, forced it open. The massive interior, barely discernable under the vanishing twilight, revealed a place unkempt and aged by time. Roger, close behind, cleared his throat.

Sebastian pulled out a box of matches from a pocket in his overcoat, removed one, and lighted a candle that sat on a nearby table. The flame hesitated under the draft before glowing brightly as soon as the door closed. Roger scrunched up his nose, his disapproval clearly written on his face.

"Age does have a unique odor," Sebastian said as he briskly rubbed hands over the dancing flame. "After a while, you get used to it."

"No electric service?"

"It was my grandfather's house. Like the Amish, he wanted separation from the world—a non-conformist at heart."

"Was?"

"He recently passed and willed the house to me."

Roger moved to the opposite side of the flickering candle. With open palms, he drew closer to its warmth. "I don't know why you brought me here on such a cold evening."

"I felt what I have to show you couldn't wait."

"What do you mean *couldn't wait?*" Roger said, voicing his annoyance. "I'm sure this could have waited for a warmer day."

"Not really. What I have to show you will mystify and scare you."

"Scare me?" Roger's hands paused near the flame. "Is there an element of danger in this?"

"There's an element of danger in everything we do, my good man. Life is full of surprises. I am about to show you one that will amaze your sense of reality."

Roger saw a smile grow on Sebastian's face and sensed some maleficence in his toothy grin.

"Are you afraid, Roger?"

“Ah … no, I’m not afraid. And stop trying to frighten me.” Roger withdrew his hands from the candle’s warmth and shoved them deep into his coat pockets. “Show me what is so important that you couldn’t have waited.”

“Follow me.” Sebastian removed the candle from the table and began to walk into the main hall. The flame danced wildly with each step, causing the shadows to frolic madly along the walls. They stopped at the base of the stairway. “What I have to show you is on the second floor.”

The stairs groaned under their weight. Roger moved to the side, grasping the railing for stability and followed. “Frankly, Sebastian, I am surprised at your civility toward me, considering my engagement to Cynthia.”

Keeping a step ahead, Sebastian let out a dismissive laugh. “Let bygones be bygones. The better man won.”

“I’m glad you feel that way. I doubt our partnership could survive if you were to hold onto any bitterness concerning Cynthia and myself.”

Sebastian paused on the landing and abruptly turned. Roger, not expecting the suddenness of the action, stepped back. Unsteadily balancing himself on the edge of the landing, he frantically reached out to grab the extended hand of his business partner. The flame on the candle faltered nearly to the point of extinguishment.

“Thank you,” Roger said, moving farther onto the ledge.

“You see, if I harbored any ill-will, I wouldn’t have taken your hand. Now, let’s get on with this. Come, we’re almost there.”

Both men resumed their climb, with Sebastian in the lead.

“I have to say,” Roger began, “the suspense is unsettling. Why can’t you tell me? And, why did you keep the passing of your grandfather a secret?”

Reaching the second floor, Sebastian moved unhurriedly to his right. “My grandfather had some … ahh, very unusual friends. Because of that, the funeral was private. And concerning my secretiveness, it’s hard to explain. It is one of those things that you need to see for yourself.”

Roger’s unease continued to grow. “You certainly have piqued my interest.”

“It’s behind this door,” Sebastian said as he gripped the handle. The hinges squealed as if to complain about being disturbed at such a late hour.

Roger hesitated. The chamber ahead was dark, and the flame from the candle appeared absorbed in the perceived enormity of the room. Only Sebastian’s highlighted profile remained visible, leaving the rest of him swallowed in the room’s blackness. “Roger, close the door behind you.”

Again, the hinges proclaimed their disapproval. The room became tomb-like in its chilling silence. The light from the candle flickered ever so slightly. Its glow refused or was unable to go beyond the immediate area.

“See that?” Sebastian whispered.

“See what?”

“The reflection of the candle at the other end of the room.”

“The …” Roger hesitated. “Yes, I see it. It’s slight, but I can make it out. You, yourself, referred to it as a reflection. I wouldn’t exactly call that unusual. Move the candle.”

Sebastion lifted the light, and in the distance, the glow mirrored his action.

“So, this is what you wanted me to see?” Roger laughed. “Again, it’s nothing more than a reflection? Is this the mystery that you couldn’t explain without us having to venture out on this cold night?”

“I’m not done. I want you to walk to the reflection while I stay here.”

“Do I get to hold the candle?”

“No. I’ll keep it. All you have to do is walk toward it.”

“Sounds easy enough.”

“Yes, it is,” Sebastion agreed and gave Roger an encouraging pat on his back.

Roger began to move forward. Without the benefit of illumination to guide him, he warily shuffled along, fixing his path solely upon the pinpoint of light. He stopped and looked back at the candle. It hovered in the midair, appearing suspended without any hint of Sebastion. “Can you hear me?” Roger called out.

Although barely perceivable, Sebastion countered, “Yes.”

Roger sensed he was moving farther away from his starting point, but not gaining on his destination. He redoubled his pace, yet nothing seemed to change. Angered by the apparent deception and trickery of Sebastion, Roger turned back, thinking this an obvious hoax perpetrated at his expense. As he turned, the faint light from the candle disappeared. Only blackness remained. He became disorientated and felt dizzy.

“Sebastion?” he cried out.

Only silence.

Oddly, when he spun around to what he perceived to be his objective, the light remained. Infuriated at the apparent ruse, Roger, in panic, began to move more quickly toward the reflection or source—confused, he didn’t know which.

“Sebastion!”

Roger’s exclamation, lost in the unfathomable void, remained unanswered.

Continuing to focus on the seemingly elusive light, he now found himself gaining on his objective. At last, it was within his grasp. No longer a reflection, it appeared to be the original candle, resting on a similar-looking table, as when he first entered the house.

“Roger, come inside,” Sebastion commanded mockingly from behind a door.

Holding the candle high in one hand, Roger gripped the handle of the door and cautiously started to enter. The chamber was dark. Once inside, the door thundered shut behind him. The brief draft from the slamming door extinguished the flame, leaving Roger immersed in blackness.

"Sebastion?"

Sebastion's baleful laughter gradually faded as the spectral darkness of the room steadily consumed Roger's sanity.

Christopher Malinger

Christopher Malinger, a native of Wisconsin, began his writing career as a public affairs reporter for the U.S. Army. After retirement, he followed his dream and began writing fictional stories encompassing most genres. He lives in Central Florida with his wife, Eileen.

Behind Closed Doors

Zak Porter did not come to school on Monday, January 9th. I remember because it was the day after my twelfth birthday party. Zak didn't say anything about skipping school. In fact, he said, "See you tomorrow, dude."

Mrs. Norris, our homeroom teacher, asked me, "Did Zak miss the bus this morning, Trevor?"

"Yeah."

"Not like him." She walked away shaking her head.

Zak and I are best friends. We met the first day of sixth grade when he sat next to me. Mrs. Norris asked Zak if he had paper and pencil.

"No, ma'am. I didn't think we'd be doing anything important," he said. That's when I laughed which caused Mrs. Norris to send me to time out. Zak gave me a mischievous 'gotcha' grin, and from that moment on, we were best friends.

At lunchtime, I texted him. *What's up? U sick?* But he didn't text back.

After school, I told Mom what happened. "I'll call his mom. I haven't talked to her in a while. Hope he's OK." Her voice faded out as she searched in her purse for her cell phone.

Dad came home at his usual time, put his briefcase on the kitchen table, and said, "Guess who visited me today?" His fists on his waist.

Mom kissed him on the cheek. "No clue, dear."

"Who, Dad?"

"The police. Seems Zak is missing."

Mom nodded. "Trevor said he didn't attend school today and I called his house, but no one answered."

Dad relayed his meeting with the police. "Did Zak act strange at your party yesterday? Did he say anything unusual?"

"No, Dad. He was Zak. You know. Just Zak. Why did the police come to see you?"

"Seems Mrs. Norris gave them my name because I coach your Little League team. Zak's on the team, ergo, I get called."

"Ergo?"

"That's intelligent talk for figure it out."

"Enough you two." Mom carried a pot of hot spaghetti to the table. "Take your stuff off the table, intelligent ones, and let's eat."

That night, before I turned off the bed light, I texted Zak again. *Where r u, dude?*

I didn't hear from Zak for two days. I even went to his house, but it was dark. Mrs. Norris stopped asking me if I had heard from Zak, and Mom just shook her head whenever I mentioned how odd it seemed.

On the third day, the police found Zak's body. When Mom told me, it felt like a punch to my stomach. I just knew it couldn't be true. "They identified the wrong body. It's not Zak." Mom said nothing, pulled me to her and hugged me for what seemed an eternity. Mom didn't let me go to school that day.

At dinner that night I turned to dad. "I don't understand. Why Zak?"

"No one knows. The paper said the police suspect his father strangled him."

"But why? They seemed happy, didn't they?'

Dad put his fork down and sipped his iced tea. "I've been thinking about that. I remember Zak coming over here to play and spend the night. But he never invited you to his house. And the only time we saw his mother was at a school event or Little League game. It's a puzzle, all right."

"Why? Were they weird or something?"

"Some people put on a good show. A good face. They cover up what's really going on in their lives."

Mom handed me the mashed potatoes. "Eat your food."

"You mean they lied?"

Dad took a bite of his meatloaf. "People hide… no, that's not right. They give an impression of one thing to hide another."

"I don't understand."

Mom placed her hand on my arm. "People present a fantasy to the outside world when their real world is broken. They wear a mask, you see."

I gave that some thought. "Oh, they pretend. But, how do you know what's real?"

My parents looked at each other. "We're having a hard time with what happened to Zak, too, dear. Eat your food," Mom repeated.

I struggled to reconstruct the clues that led to my belief that Zak's life was a happy one. I realized that I never met his father. Was that part of the mystery? Yes, Dad was right about never being invited to his house. In fact, when I would go there, Zak would always walk outside, close the door behind him, and say, "Let's go to your house." That was it. Two clues. The picture of the perfect, loving family was fake – a fantasy, as Mom put it.

The news reports over the next week revealed fragments about Zak's dad, like the fact that he was unemployed even though Zak told everyone he was a computer expert working from home. TV reporters also told how Mr. Porter covered up his financial problems with counterfeit checks and fake loans. He even stole a new Mercedes from a dealer lot in another city.

When the police finally located Mr. Porter, he had a suitcase full of cash and a passport in another name. I wondered if Porter was his real name. He told the police that his wife killed Zak, but I didn't believe that. Nobody believed that.

With Mr. Porter in jail and Mrs. Porter missing, no one claimed Zak's body, so they didn't hold a funeral. My Dad and several Little League parents chipped in to pay the cost of cremation and burial. No one talked about Zak after that. No one.

Several months following Mr. Porter's arrest, Dad and I were sitting at the kitchen table waiting for Mom to finish cooking dinner. I was doing my homework while Dad read the paper.

"I don't think Zak was part of this con game everyone talked about."

He peered at me over the paper. "What makes you say that?"

"Because he wasn't fake with me. Our friendship felt real."

He put the paper down. "I'm sure you and Zak were best buds. You miss him, don't you?"

I nodded.

"Things aren't always what they seem, son. You've learned a hard lesson in a most horrendous way."

***

I'm older now but I think of Zak Porter often. I still ask "why." Maybe Zak wanted a perfect family and worked to make everyone, including me, believe the illusion. Did Zak want out of the con? Did Mr. Porter kill Zak because he felt his secret would be revealed? There were so many lies; it was difficult to sort out the truth.

Over the years, I've met many people who deceive, who pretend they're something, or someone else. They give one impression to the world but inside they agonize. Zak was my first.

What did Shakespeare write? *To thine own self be true*. I didn't understand that quote when I was young. Now I realize that living a true life is hard. I'm still developing, still striving to be true to myself. Zak didn't get that chance, and I often wonder who Zak would have become.

Arleen Mariotti

Arleen is a retired teacher. She has published three work texts and several short stories. She is an adjunct instructor at Hillsborough Community College, and volunteers to teach art at senior living facilities.

A Grand Illusion

Entering the Las Vegas Pinnacle Hotel, Bonnie could not avoid the large electronic signs advertising that night's main event: "The Grand Illusionist, 9 pm, Starlight Theater." Her husband's picture loomed large in the advertisement, with his trademark cape and magician's hat.

I'd like to throw a brick at his mug. Fourteen years with him and I'm only now wising up. She took the elevator to their 22nd floor suite, and used her room card to enter.

What will I find now? Another honey?

Howard looked up from the couch, where he had been reading a newspaper. "Bonnie, what brings you back so soon? Thought you weren't returning until later?"

"After my gym workout, I decided to skip the movie. I have a headache and want to lie down. Is the bed free?"

"What kind of question is that?"

"What kind of husband would sleep with his mistress while his wife is working out at the gym?"

"We've gone over this. I was wrong, and I admitted it."

"You admitted it once because I caught you. How about all the other times?"

"She is not my mistress."

"No, just your stage assistant. Easily available. And you, the so-called Grand Illusionist. When I walked in on you last week, why didn't you make her disappear, like you do on the stage?"

"Bonnie, give me a break. My show starts in just two hours. Let's not argue now, please?"

"They pay you fifty grand a night here at the Pinnacle. Not bad for two hours."

"Why the hell are you bringing that up?"

"Where's the money?"

"I don't understand your question."

"Let's see, a four-week stint in Vegas twice a year, six shows a week, that's three hundred thousand times eight, or two point four million, if my math is correct. Not to mention your other shows in New York and Atlantic City. Where's all the money?"

"What the hell are you talking about? Does your credit card bounce when you go shopping?"

"No, but the money is nowhere to be found. It's not in our joint account."

"I've told you before, my agent handles it. It's in his account, under my name."

"Is your agent in the Cayman Islands?"

"What?"

"You heard me. Georgetown, Grand Cayman. I know all about it. If we get divorced, which you know damn well is coming, there won't be any estate to split. It's hidden. Off shore. And worse, dear, when the money is ultimately found, the IRS will get it all, for past taxes. And your ass will be in jail."

"I've paid all my taxes. Where do you come up with these crazy accusations?"

"Sorry, Howard, won't wash. You have lived up to your billing. The Grand Illusionist, indeed. You've made the money disappear. But if your wife can't get her share in court, I'm sure the IRS will. Your tricks might fool the Starlight Theater crowd, but not me. At least not the ones in real life."

"This is utter nonsense. You have no evidence."

"Oh, yes I do. I'm not always in the gym, or out shopping. I've been investigating. Or paying someone who knows how to find information."

"Like what?"

"Like, what about Melissa Jane Singleton?"

Oh, his pained expression! He's guilty as hell. Gotcha!

"Sorry, Howard. I didn't hear your answer. Well, let me answer for you. A few months ago, you paid her a cool fifty thousand to keep quiet about your affair. She threatened to ruin your show. All documented."

"That's a lie!"

"Deny what you will. It'll all come out in court."

"It's not fair to bring all this up just now. Be fair, Bonnie, and stop with these crazy accusations. I have a show to do tonight."

He doesn't want to go on stage feeling my anger. That's good.

"You probably can do the show in your sleep, so no need to worry. I need some fresh air. If you want to discuss this further, get up off the couch. I'll be out on the balcony."

She opened the sliding doors and entered the suite's narrow balcony. The sun had set, making the nighttime view spectacular, with brightly-lit casinos up and down Las Vegas Boulevard. She found the cool air refreshing. She leaned against the four-foot high wall of the balcony to get the best view and called out, "It's a great view tonight, Howard. I can see all the way to downtown Vegas."

He came out to the balcony, stood a few feet to her right and stared into the night. "Bonnie, I don't want you to be angry with me. Let me get through my show tonight and we can discuss all this later. I promise I can explain everything."

The man lies, then lies some more.

"I'm worried, Howard. After all, you are The Grand Illusionist. You can make anything disappear. Maybe even including me."

"What the hell are you talking about? Now you're getting really crazy. I would never harm you."

"Okay, maybe I'm being a bit unfair. But you can see why I get so upset. A man who cheats on his wife can do anything."

"I said I'm sorry. Can't we let it go?"

"All right, fair enough. For now. Please hold me. It's a little chilly."

He walked over and put his arms around her. "So, can we be friends again? Maybe lovers tonight, after the show?"

He has barely touched me in bed the last two weeks. What a phony!

"Yes, that would be good. I'll be in bed, waiting for you."

He relaxed his grip and kissed her on the lips. She returned the kiss.

Now he's happy. Off guard. She let go of an object from one hand. "I dropped the barrette from my hair. Let me get it."

She bent down to the balcony floor to find the barrette. Near the floor she inserted her head and shoulders between his thighs and the balcony wall, grabbed his ankles with both hands and lifted him with surprising ease, angling him toward the wall.

Not as heavy as I thought.

"What are you doing?" he cried as she stood, raising his body higher and higher. His arms flailed in the air but could not reach her. She angled his legs up so his torso now extended over the wall – and let go.

Well, Mr. Illusionist, you had one too many illusions: that you could get away with your deceits. My gym time was well spent. Amazing what 125 pounds can do with someone 50 pounds heavier.

She quickly re-entered the suite, closed the door to the balcony and walked toward the desk phone.

Now to call the front desk, report his suicide. There is no note, but he had plenty of reasons to leap over the balcony. A divorce he did not want.

Soon-to-be-discovered tax fraud. Probably other mistresses seeking to extort. Justice at last!

She reached for the receiver, ready to press the button and tell her story. Just then, in the dim light, her eye caught a slight movement from across the room. *No!*

"Did you have fun out there, Bonnie?" The voice was unmistakable. And he was still sitting on the couch.

Lawrence Martin

Larry is a retired physician, past president of Writers League of The Villages, FL, and past RPLA winner for short stories, middle-grade fiction and historical fiction. His writing covers several genres, and includes books for both adults and kids.

The Last Coupon

“You don’t have enough points, sir.” John locked eyes with the young man. “Could I please speak to Mr. Jarvis?” ”He’s at the County Building meeting with Mr. Clark from the Office of Price Administration.”

Damn the OPA, and damn those Nazi bastards to Hell.

“I just need a pound of sugar and a lousy can of pineapple for my wife. Is that too much to ask?”

“Sorry, sir. I could lose my job, even go to jail if I ignore the rules. You’ll be eligible for a new ration book in ten days.”

“My son ships out for Europe day after tomorrow. He’s getting married tonight, and his mother is set on baking him a wedding cake, and his favorite is pineapple upside-down. I’m only ten points shy.”

The clerk remained silent.

“Damned war has taken everything.” John dropped his gaze and stomped toward the door. “Took my brother and my best friend. Can’t drive my car because I can’t get a tire to replace the flat and now...”

He slammed the screen door behind him. His shoulder collided with someone. He looked up into the face of a gray-haired lady he’d seen in church a few times. “I’m sorry, I wasn’t looking.”

She smiled. “That’s okay, Mr. Markey.”

As he tipped his hat and started to step around her, she said, “You’re a deacon at the church, ain’t you?”

“Yes, Mrs....”

“Taylor, Mary Taylor.”

“I’m so sorry, Mary. I’m not in a fit mood right now, but I should have said hello just the same.”

“I couldn’t help but overhear your conversation with the clerk.” John’s face reddened.

“Don’t mind me hearin’ the rough language. Me mister, God rest his soul, could say a might worse when things went wrong.”

"I should set a better example."

"Yer human, just like the rest of us. I don't 'spect God will hold a few damns against you. Especially given the targets." Mary took out a small yellow envelope and pulled off the last page from the pack within it. "You take it, and get what yer Mrs. needs."

"That's very kind of you, but—"

Her hand on his arm stopped his next word. "I'm old, and I've got no one else to help."

"I can't take your last slip. You came in to buy—"

"Pish-tosh, Mr. Markey. God knows, I don't really need anything this ticket can buy, and what you need won't wait."

John reached out a shaking hand, took the ticket, hugged Mary, and went back inside.

"Here!" He shoved his ticket and Mary's across the counter. A few minutes later, he scooped up his package and hurried home.

John set the sugar and can of pineapple on the kitchen table just as his wife, Helen, came in the back door. Her eyes opened wide. "How did you get those? We didn't have enough points." She dropped her sweater on the counter. "You didn't buy tickets from someone? Oh, John, you'll get in trouble and—"

"Don't worry, dear. I was on my way to do that very thing when someone from church gave me a ticket. She heard me arguing with the clerk. I wouldn't have taken it because it was her last one, but she insisted."

"What a wonderful thing to do." Helen went to the cupboard and took out her largest mixing bowl. "Who was she?"

"Mary Taylor."

Helen's knees buckled, and she dropped onto one of the kitchen chairs. "That can't be, John." She shook her head and clutched at her chest.

"But it was. She told me her name herself."

"John." Helen took in a deep breath. "Mary Taylor died three days ago."

Robert E. Marvin

Robert is a member of Florida Writers, FWA Manatee Chapter. His short stories have appeared in the FWA anthologies and FWA magazines. He was a finalist in the Apparitionist National Ghost Story competition and received awards from Writer Advice and Writer's Type.

GRAY RIDER

Craig Needham perused the attic over his grandmother's garage in Brattleboro, Vermont. He visited his hometown to attend the twenty-fifth high school reunion of Brattleboro High. The next day, the gathering would be held in the school's gymnasium. But this night, he was alone in the sprawling 1876 Victorian house. Craig disagreed with his brother and sister's decision to sell the place when Grandma Beatrice passed away last year since the family built the home ninety-five years ago.

He yanked the pull chain for the single overhead light. Memories rushed at him, almost too fast to process. Craig found New England antiques covered with dust and the musty smell of a long-abandoned room: an old leather trunk now peeling after years of dry weather and heat, a Red Warrior Sled, the best in its day, but no longer manufactured, stacks of first print classic books, skis that had cut swaths through Mount Snow many times, and an old Royal typewriter he hammered away on as a ten-year-old when he looked for something to do with his hands.

Grandpa's favorite bicycle looked old and in need of a friend. The brand name, Graybar Roadrunner became scratched and reduced to *Gray ba*. Rust encrusted the sprockets and chains. Craig felt a kinship with the old Gray Rider. He found an oil can, sprayed over the rust, and spun the wheels. They turned freely, seeming happy to come alive. "Voilà," Craig shouted. *Why not take it for a ride?* he thought.

He pedaled up Western Avenue to Canal Street and traveled over the covered bridge near Dunfy's General Store. The cool, fall air engulfed Craig. Nostalgia wrapped him up sparked by the sight of mountains bursting with vibrant red and yellow colors of autumn. He pulled up to the house just as night cast its cloak over Brattleboro. Craig felt like a boy again as he returned the bike to its berth in the garage attic.

At 7 a.m., his alarm clock jolted him awake. With the reunion scheduled for 6 p.m., Craig felt eager to check out the house to insure it looked ready to appeal to potential buyers. First, he needed his daily two-mile run. He slipped into his sweats and burst out the front door onto the front porch; he stopped abruptly. There on the front lawn was Gray Rider. He tried to remember the night before. Craig was sure he returned the bike to the attic, recalling how he turned off the light on his way out. Confused, he carried the bike upstairs.

***

At the reunion, Craig enjoyed seeing the faces of old friends as they retold stories of their youthful escapades. He noticed a lot of gray hair, pot bellies, makeup, and wrinkled faces.

When Craig returned home at 12:32 a.m., he felt his heartbeat quicken. Out on the lawn sat Gray Rider. Either someone used the bike, or played a trick on Craig, or he had too much Jack Daniels at the reunion. He remembered bringing Gray Rider upstairs that morning.

Sweat ran down Craig's face although the air had ushered a deep autumn chill. He loosened his collar, removed his tie, and straddled the bicycle to ride it back to the garage, but it wouldn't budge. Then Gray Rider drove onto Western Avenue on its own accord. Several pedestrians didn't seem to notice him. Like a scene from a science fiction thriller, storefronts and houses had changed appearances or disappeared entirely. Time reversed to earlier years in Brattleboro–fifty, a hundred years ago, or more. The scene warped to a bright, warm, summer day.

Craig waved at the townsfolk, but no one acknowledged him. No cars existed; the road was just a dusty dirt street. Gray Rider took him on a tour of the past–the early 1800s.

Where Stockwell's Eatery now stood, Craig saw a store selling saddles and farm equipment. A blacksmith's shop occupied the property where currently a Shell Gas Station stood. But Gray Rider had no intention of making this a pleasure outing.

Passing the local New England Bank, Craig heard gunfire and witnessed a bank robbery. He recalled this was the biggest bank heist of all time, dubbed the Big Bank Burner by the local newspaper. The thieves were never apprehended. Looking closely, Craig saw they were four young, teenage boys and one girl, looking much like grownups. No wonder they had never been caught. They grew up in their hometown, hiding in plain sight.

Gray Rider veered to the cemetery. Craig witnessed something never reported. With Mrs. Lighthall present, he saw groundskeepers dig to exhume Dr. Lighthall's body for whatever reason, and they discovered his grave was empty. Mrs. Lighthall's heart stopped from the emotional impact. Why did he abandon her?

"Her heart just stopped beating," the coroner said, "and her eyes locked open in fright." Time morphed to the day of her burial. Craig watched as they buried her with her secret.

Time changed again. Gray Rider cycled to Main Street where a wedding was taking place at the First Congregational Church. Craig had attended this church into adulthood. Horse-drawn carriages lined the crowded road; townsfolk dressed in their Sunday best. Gray Rider stopped in front of its sign on the lawn which announced the wedding of Mr. Jared Stone to Miss Mildred Haley. Shocked, Craig recognized the bride as his mother, Mildred, but Jared Stone wasn't his father. Craig noticed he resembled Mr. Stone–tall, broad shouldered, sandy-reddish hair, blue eyes, and heavy, bushy eyebrows. Craig's friends always chided him about his brows; Craig Highbrow became his street name.

But Mom was a Needham, married to his dad, a banker, Harold Needham. Craig smiled. "Mom," he said to no one, "you hid your family secret well. You remarried and gave me the Needham name. That's okay with me." He gazed up toward heaven. Gray Rider's tour of Brattleboro became a ticket to unwritten history.

Soon Craig found himself on the lawn in front of his grandmother's house straddling Gray Rider. "What just happened? What do I do with this sordid new information?" Questions with no answers were impossible to ponder. He needed some sleep for the drive home the next day.

Craig rode Gray Rider to the garage, carried it up the stairwell, placed it in its berth, and chained it to an exposed beam. He turned off the lights, left, and locked the door.

At 7 a.m., his alarm shocked him awake. He didn't have a hangover but almost. Craig grabbed a cup of coffee and bounced out the front door. Gray Rider was nowhere in sight. He turned 360 degrees to make sure. He still couldn't make sense of the events the night before. Did he really learn the identities of the robbers? Why did Mr. Lighthall bolt? Was he really Craig Stone, not Craig Needham? Or did he dream this, riding down a river of Jack Daniels Whiskey?

Craig began his morning jog, while Gray Rider rested in the garage attic, somehow looking better for wear.

Frank T. Masi

Frank T. Masi is the editor of *The Typewriter Legend.* His writing appears in business publications, Florida Writers Association collections, *The Florida Writer*, and *Not Your Mother's Book.* His poetry is in *Revelry*, Florida State Poets Association anthologies, and *Looking Life in the Eye, Poets of Central Florida, Volume Three.*

THE OTHER SIDE

By now the sense of wrongness tickled up her neck like a trail of ants. Jazz grabbed the rearview; opened her mouth, stuck out her tongue. "Ahhh."

"Nope. No mirrors." Sally slapped her hand away and repositioned the mirror. "You drive. I'll check." Sally's voice sounded tinny and brittle. Her best friend since forever reached over from the passenger seat and felt Jazz's cheek. "A tad warm. No big whoop."

"You don't feel that?" Jazz focused the A/C vents on her face and breathed in.

"By *that* you mean—?"

"Everything's wrong, Sal. You, me, *this*. Air doesn't have enough, I don't know, oxygen?" She glanced left at Sally's raised eyebrows. No help there.

"You're fighting it again," Sally said. "Stop it. Remember, they drive on the left here."

"I know. That's not—"

"You'll get used to it."

"Everything's backwards."

"So? Steering wheel, gearshift, friggin' radio—on the left. Shift with your left hand. Problem solved—"

A car horn blared on their right. Jazz quick-corrected and wrestled to center the squirming car.

"—If you don't kill us first. Want me to drive? I've been here longer than you."

"No, no. I'm fine." She gripped the wheel tight with both hands. "Getting the hang of this backwards stuff already. I can feel it."

"Seriously?" Sally snapped her seatbelt in place and the metallic click hung in the air like a loud question mark.

"Cross my heart." Jazz thought for two seconds and crossed her left hand on the right side of her chest. "See?"

Sally chuckled. "That's my girl."

Ten minutes later they arrived without incident and Jazz breathed a silent prayer of thanks. The drive over was tough. But that would be nothing compared to the minefield ahead. She shifted into PARK and undid the belt. She looked over to see Sally staring at her. Concern shadowed every crease in her friend's forehead.

"What?"

"Your mom wants to show off her new boyfriend, that's all." Sally reached over and brushed back Jazz's bangs. "You can do this."

"Easy for you to say."

"Easy for you to do. Now let's go. We're being watched. I just saw the curtains move."

Jazz led the way up the front steps and the door snatched open before her finger reached the doorbell.

"Jazzy, honey. Give Momma a hug."

Her mother rushed forward with a click-clack of high heels and outstretched arms. Jazz had no choice but to return the neck-wring in reflex. Her mother's trademark Chanel wrapped her in a cloying flowery cloud that scared off every oxygen molecule in a five-foot circumference.

Sally, bless her, came to her rescue and pried Jazz free. Her friend slipped in and took up where Jazz left off, pressing cheeks with her mother and gently turning the woman so Jazz could get in a few much needed, surreptitious gulps of air.

"Mrs. Hopkins, so good to see you again! You always give the best hugs. How about one more? It's been so long."

"Why, aren't you a treasure Sally! You have always been my favorite of all Jazz's friends."

Jazz caught Sally's eye over her mom's shoulder and stretched an imaginary hangman's rope up high. She cocked her head and thrust her tongue out to the side. Sally hid her chuckle with a cough and the two women separated.

"Well," Jazz's mom patted her dress and smoothed her hair, "much as I'd like to, I can't keep you girls to myself. There's someone inside I want you to meet and afterwards, I have big news!" The woman clapped hands like a little girl excited about a new puppy. "Come, come." She opened the door with a flourish and whisked them in.

Jazz took one step inside and stopped short. Sally's nose bumped the back of Jazz's head.

"Ouch, dammit Jazz." Sally shoved her forward, stepped in, and halted. "Whoa, hello everybody. Looks like a party."

Indeed it did. A banner—*Congratulations Melinda and Ben!*—sagged over the dining room entrance. A dozen people juggling drinks and paper plates grazed around a buffet table crowded with platters and casseroles, chips and dips.

Standing at the front of the crowd, a sweaty man in a too-tight polo shirt inched forward, shifted a plate and can of beer to one hand and extended the other. It took Jazz a full second to register that the fat, freckled hand hanging in mid-air was the man's left.

She took it, also with her left hand and dropped it quickly. She glanced at the banner and plastered on a smile. "You must be Ben," she said.

Jazz's mother hurried up beside the man and leaned into him, clasping swooning hands to her chest. "Yes, yes. This is Ben. Isn't he just the bomb? Do you kids still say that? *The bomb?*"

Sally clamped a hand on Jazz's shoulder and squeezed hard. "Sometimes, Mrs. H, we even say bomb-diggity. To make it special."

Jazz turned to her friend and Sally's laughing eyes defused the smart remark hanging back on Jazz's tongue. She swallowed and leaned forward. "Hello there, um, Mr. Bomb Diggity. I'm Jazz and this joker beside me is my best friend, Sally. I'm guessing you are half of the surprise my mother has cooked up for us?"

"Isn't she precious, Ben? I told you." She hip-checked the man for emphasis and sloshed a splash of foam from his beer. "And so smart. The other half? Is right here!" Her mother extended a hand, her right hand, and wagged the finger sporting a diamond large enough to choke a goose. "We're engaged! Can you believe it?"

Jazz could, actually. This would be her mother's third marriage after Dad. But who's counting? She tapped the beer can in Ben's fist. "Any more where that came from?"

"Outside fridge," he exhaled as some of the worry melted from his face. "Garage."

***

In the car on the way home, Jazz chewed her lips and concentrated on driving. *Stay left. Stay left*. Three beers weren't a lot, but she was still getting used to being here. No sense pushing her luck.

"You did awesome, girl," Sally said. "Like you belonged here. I thought the ring thing might blow your cool, wrong hand, wrong finger, you know. But, nope, you sailed right on past that."

"Why shouldn't I? None of that back there mattered, Sally. She's not my mother."

"Now, Jazz. We talked about this."

"She's a reflection of my mother. That's what you said when you talked me into stepping across. Come with me, Jazz. You'll like it here. *Everything's the same, only backwards. You said that*."

"I had to tell you something. Otherwise, you'd have stayed on your side, sick as you were, and died before you crossed."

"You died," Jazz said.

Sally nodded. "Like you."

"Then how—?"

"My reflection got lonely for yours." Sally shrugged. "I pulled some strings."

"*Mirror, mirror on the wall*? Dude, I'm living it. High five. *Left* hand."

"It's not a joke, Jazz. Mirrors are *different* on this side. Promise me?"

"What?"

"You won't look at yourself in any mirrors here? Swear it. It's important."

"But why—?"

"You won't like what you see."

Mark McWaters

Mark McWaters has an MFA in Creative Writing from the University of North Carolina, is an award-winning Advertising Creative Director, a previous #1 and #2 winner in Collections, a multiple RPLA Short Fiction winner and a First Place RPLA winner for unpublished novel in both Thriller and YA categories.

GHOST WRITER

Navy SEALs, SWAT teams, and mystery writers like me relied on situational awareness. The five police SUVs parked outside the hotel were my first clues the conference would be unlike any I'd attended previously. I hesitated, debating whether it was safe to go inside. People weren't running away and I didn't hear gunfire, so I decided to check in.

Floral perfume enveloped a dark-haired beauty ahead of me in line. She was a best-selling author friend who always knew the answers to whatever was important.

I tapped her shoulder. "Hey, Marla, any idea why the cops are here?"

She turned and whispered, "Dead body in one of the rooms—possibly a homicide."

"On opening day at a mystery conference? Talk about irony! Some of our author friends will be disappointed they missed it this year."

As the line progressed, I spotted crime-scene techs covered in white paper suits striding through the lobby.

Murder indeed.

I grabbed my key card and dragged my roller case to room 566, which turned out to be directly beneath the one with the dead body. I knew this fact because all the entry doors faced an interior courtyard. The glass elevator had given me an excellent view of my room and the one above it, where police stood at guard.

After unpacking I located the convention area and picked up my identification badge and program. Later I met friends for our yearly dinner. The authors expressed a macabre fascination with the alleged crime.

"You've heard of murder-mystery dinners," Paulette said. "At first I thought it was something like that, you know, staged for opening night."

Dan said, "I talked to one of the detectives. Definitely a criminal investigation. I never thought I'd attend an event that started with a real whodunnit. You can't make this stuff up."

I took a deep drink of merlot. "There was nothing about it on the six o'clock news."

"The hotel probably wants it kept quiet. Murder is bad for business," Ariana, a lawyer turned author, said between sips of chardonnay.

Dan chuckled. "Not during a mystery writers conference."

Lorna swirled her martini. "I bet his wife caught him cheating and popped him."

"You could be right," I said. "The CSIs were still collecting evidence when I stopped by my room before dinner."

Our kindred group enjoyed drinking, dining, and speculating about the investigation. Much later we retired to our rooms, anticipating a long weekend of educational activities.

***

The next two days were a blur of writing workshops, lively cocktail parties, and dinner conversations with experienced authors and eager newbies.

By midnight on Saturday night, I was exhausted and feeling a little tipsy. I sat on the edge of the bed in my two-room suite and pulled the dressy black sandal off my left foot.

That was when I saw them: people silently streaming in from my left and right.

I was certain I'd locked the door.

The unexpected visitors startled me. My heart rate soared.

None of them looked at me. They acted like I wasn't there.

Confused, I jumped up. "Who are you people?"

No response.

I froze.

The men and women looked normal, wearing typical clothing for March in South Florida. They searched my room with single-minded intensity.

Something even more shocking happened next. The people on either side of me reached my center of vision and vanished.

Huh? Had I imagined them? I was tired and under the influence of some excellent merlot.

I glanced around the room.

Everyone was gone.

I must've been dreaming.

Relaxed again and half asleep, I sat back down and pulled off my other shoe.

The same people appeared once more.

This time I paid closer attention. They seemed to be walking, but they didn't have visible lower legs or feet.

Holy mother—

It wasn't a dream. I was wide awake.

Like before, the intruders disappeared the second they reached my center of vision.

Adrenaline fired up enough of my brain cells to overcome the effects of the merlot.

Must be ghosts. Maybe they're looking for the dead guy's spirit. But why look in my room? Were they given the wrong room number?

I'd never seen spirits before. I wasn't expecting them to look like live people with the exception of the missing lower limbs. The ghosts didn't scare me, because heavy wine consumption had short-circuited my brain's common-sense and fear functions. Instead I found the situation weirdly humorous.

Note to self: Drink less wine.

I was so tired I could barely keep my eyes open. The spectral visitors hadn't shown an interest in me, so I undressed, turned off the light, and fell asleep.

When I went to the lobby to get breakfast the next morning, I bumped into the shaman I'd met at a paranormal workshop the day before. She wore a gossamer green dress that hugged her curves and caressed her ankles.

"Hey, Yoni, you'll never believe what happened to me last night." I told her everything.

She nodded. "Definitely searching for the waylaid spirit. Ghosts always appear in your peripheral vision, usually when you're in a semiconscious state of deep relaxation. The lost spirit must've left his room, forcing them to search the entire hotel."

When I told my colleagues about my late-night visitors, most of them shook their heads and assumed I'd drunk too much wine.

Lorna, who admitted she'd seen spirits before, told me the ghost posse had followed her out to the parking lot the previous night.

The spirit squad's inability to find the missing soul surprised me. Their incompetence could result in their having to search the entire city. The poor guy might never be found.

I pondered his fate during my drive home.

***

A month later I returned to the hotel for a luncheon, and an employee told me there had been several ghost sightings since my last visit.

Maybe the recovery team would've had better luck if it had split up instead of searching as a group. I assumed time wasn't an issue for them. Judging by the stressed-out looks I'd seen on their faces a month earlier, they took their jobs seriously. I wondered if they would still be looking for the wandering spirit when the mystery writers conference returned to the hotel the following year. Maybe I'd see them in my room again, but first I'd have to drink enough wine to simulate the same conditions. It would be a huge sacrifice, but the research could prove useful for my next paranormal mystery novel.

***

I never saw the hotel ghosts again, but the experience sharpened my senses. I became more aware of what lurked in my peripheral vision. Soon my paranormal sightings were not dependent on wine consumption, although it did help.

Residents of the spirit world fascinated me. Half asleep in my living-room recliner late at night, I glimpsed the ghost of an elderly woman who had died in my house forty years earlier. She wore a white cotton nightgown and fuzzy slippers. A whiff of her cigarette smoke lingered after our encounter.

***

This is a true story, so naturally names were changed.

Cheers!

Sharon Menear

Retired international airline Captain Sharon (S.L.) Menear draws from her varied worldwide experiences to inject realism into her fast-paced Samantha Starr thrillers and her Jett Jorgensen mysteries. She also has an anthology book: *Life, Love, & Laughter – 50 Short Stories.*

WORDS FROM THE EARTH

No sign of warming, not one degree. If anything, colder. A damp wind with sporadic light chilling rain gusted through leafless scraggly turkey oaks and scattered longleaf pines as I scurried about looking for shelter. I had made a mistake, assuming it would not be so cold in the hills of the Withlacoochee State Forest in coastal Citrus County. Yet, January is the season for volunteer geological work for the Florida Department of Forestry, mapping sinkholes. Why this time of year? Visibility is better; the leaves are gone. Moreover, the snakes are hiding, smarter than I am. If awake, they are probably watching, hissing themselves to exhaustion, laughing at me.

How long on this project? Probably six years. Florida didn't have funding to continue a forest sinkhole-mapping program. Retired, I was looking for something interesting. This and writing short stories and speculative fiction novels kept me busy. Yet, writing inspiration was slow; a day in the field would be good.

Massive Eocene to Oligocene-age limestone, intensely fractured and cavernous, underlies these rolling sand-covered hills of the Brooksville Ridge. Where sand is slowly subsiding into openings in the deeper limestone, sinkholes form. On warmer days, I would walk these woods, locating sinkholes or caves, measuring depth and width, noting where water moved downward into swallow holes, recording that information after determining precise coordinates using a hand-held GPS unit.

Not today, too cold. Pushing down a long brushy slope into a deep circular basin crammed with saw palmettoes and leg-snatching catbrier vines, high rock walls rose above me. The bone-penetrating wind did not reach the bottom. Slight rain continued.

May as well make myself useful, record what I see. This was a new sinkhole, a big one, deeper than most. It was different, with massive weathered gray limestone outcropping, forming walls at the bottom. I moved under an overhanging rock ledge, to take notes, and to get out of the rain. Stepping backward, I slipped, fell, sliding headfirst on my back on slippery clay down a narrow crevasse, bumping to an abrupt stop at the bottom.

Disturbed bats flapped above me. Then it was quiet again. Quiet and dark. Black dark. Unseen hand in front of your face dark.

Squinting, I sought the slightest hint of light coming down from the opening. Nothing! Where was it?

Light! Yes, my cellphone. The flashlight app.

Holy crap! An enormous cave. I'm not supposed to be here. The Forestry people said, "Map sinkholes, just don't go into any caves". I didn't; I fell in!

I'll crawl back up. Sweeping the cellphone about, I saw the incline, covered with clay, and signs of my slide.

Working my way upward, the end never came. I turned the light off, looking for a glow, a glimmer. Darkness. No sign of the exit. How far had I slid? Maybe this is the wrong way out. I moved back down to the big cavern. Was there another way? Did I get confused?

Swinging my light back and forth. No, that was the only way out. Try again.

However, before continuing, my light caught gleaming white calcite-covered limestone walls. Black and red outline paintings of animals covered them. Ancient bison, mammoths, a cave bear, and animals I had never seen before. No, yes I had. Southern France and Spain, places I had read about, not Florida. Yet, these creatures had been in Florida as late as 10,000 to 12,000 years ago, the last of the Ice-Age megafauna. Running my fingers across the outlines, I felt a tingle moving from fingertips to the back of my neck. Someone here?

Whipping around, no one. Looking back at the wall, a human face, looking at me. What!

It moved across the cave wall as shifting, flowing lines, like the animal figures painted on the wall with red ocher and black manganese oxides. A round-faced woman with owlish dark-framed glasses, lips moving. A deep warbling bass sound came to me, slowly increasing in pitch, then changing to words.

"You are here to be called? You want to be Zelandoni?"

"What? No," stammering. "I fell into this cave."

Laughing melodically, "Just having fun. You should see your face!"

"I know you. You are Jean Auel, the author of Clan of the Cave Bear."

"Bright fellow! So, why are you here? These caves are sacred places. You have read my books. You know the rules for being called."

"I told you; I fell in. Yes, I have read them. All of them."

"So, reading them entitles you to be called?"

"Called? I just want to get out. That hole is the one I slid down, but it doesn't lead to the top, where I fell in."

Auel looked at me, disdainfully. "Not called, no chance to be Zelandoni. Perhaps a different calling."

"I just want out!"

Calmly ignoring me, "What do you do?"

"I'm a geologist, a volunteer geologist. I'm mapping sinkholes, caves and other karst features."

An undulating laugh bounced from wall to wall in the cavern, "That's all you do, nothing of value? Just a rock whacker?"

"I write. Short stories and novels, speculative fiction, parallel universe stories, and alternate histories. Does that count for anything?"

"Why are you in this cave, pounding on rocks? Why aren't you writing?"

My flashlight dimming, I freaked out, yelling. "Get me out of here! I fell in. I want to see the sky again."

"Why aren't you writing"?

"I don't have any ideas right now. That's why I'm here, to take a break, to freshen my brain."

"Follow me," motioning toward a narrow passage I had not seen.

"My light is almost gone; I'll be lost here, forever."

Her outline changing to an almost realistic person on the wet, white calcite-covered surface, an ocher-red finger extended from the rock wall. Sizzling in the damp cave air, it touched the cellphone. The power gauge jumped.

Gawking at the phone, I followed, as she slid along the wall and into a broad crack in the rock.

Deeper into the cave system we went, arriving at a dead-end. In a low spot was a pool of water.

"Turn off your light."

The pool glowed, a clear deep blue, as of purest glacial ice.

"Look into it. What do you see?"

Bending over, my eyes plunged into a circular rock-walled blue abyss, deeper and deeper. They focused on moving groups of animals, masses of bison and mammoths, and others.

A wrinkled old man with reddish skin and long stringy black hair sat in front of a fire, throwing powder into it. Brightly colored flames surged skyward with each flicking of his fingers.

"That's what you should be doing. You are a storyteller. Go!"

Suddenly, it darkened. The blue pool was gone. I lay on the floor of the cave, cold, and smeared with wet clay. Jean Auel and the animals were gone. Flashlight dimming again, I turned it off.

Above me, up a sloping crack … a faint light. Far away. The way out!

Crawling up the narrow crevice, slipping on the clay, I reached the top. It was warmer. Blue skies!

An idea, a story.

John Charles Miller

John Charles Miller, Tampa, Florida, groundwater geologist and speculative fiction writer. Self-published works include *Citrus White Gold, The Gatherers, and Deep Florida (The Florida Time-Travel Series)*, two collections of short stories/poetry, *You Can't Pick Up Raindrops* and *He Hears the Rocks*, and a parallel universe romance novel *Dead Not Dead*.

ILLUSION OR REALITY

Pungent smells of body waste, sweat and fear fill the low-ceilinged dungeon. Incessant flickering light from torches stuck in the walls makes day and night the same, like being buried alive in a mass grave. I'm a shackled beast. My bones ache. Fury boils in my gut.

Most of us have been here only a few days, waiting for a trial to free us, or, more likely, to condemn us to death by stoning, strangulation, burning, boiling in oil, or crucifixion. I've been condemned to death, have already cut and chiseled my crossbeam.

Outside, voices grow loud enough for us to hear. "Give us Barabbas!" Then moments later, "Crucify him! Crucify him!"

I'm paralyzed with terror. I don't want to die. If I believed in a loving God, I would pray to Him to save me.

The guards' sandals slap against the ground as they march toward this subterranean hell. A rusty door screeches open. "Barabbas!" The voice is raspy like a throat lined with sand. They haul me to my feet. I scuffle between them along the low-arched passageway, my chains clanging together with each step through shadows of death.

They drag me up stone steps, the centers worn shiny. One guard unlocks my chains and shoves me toward the courtyard. The sun's glare blinds me. I squint and shield my eyes, breathe in a hint of lilies and frankincense. Crowds fill the courtyard, high priests and elders with hand-woven robes draping their heads and bodies. Some men I recognize as my comrades in battle against the Romans, their fists raised. "Barabbas! Barabbas!"

But they're smiling, laughing.

I don't understand.

I turn to the governor as he shouts toward the crowd, "But Jesus has done no harm. Why do you choose Barabbas? An insurrectionist! A convicted murderer!"

A man stands in the shadows. When sunlight touches him, he glows, then gazes at me with the illusion of unconditional love. I can't look away. Is this Jesus?

"Go," the guard yells at me, shoving me again. "You are free."

What? Then I remember. Jews can ask for the release of a prisoner sentenced to death during their Passover celebration. But why me, a heathen? Jesus is a Jew. He healed lepers and brought a dead man back to life. Talked about a loving God. Why don't they choose him?

A moment later, my comrades rush toward me and slap me on the back, embrace me, pull me into the courtyard.

We follow the crowd to where Jesus now stands tied to a post, his robe ripped from his body. A soldier, muscular arms glistening in sunlight, whips Jesus with several thongs entwined with pieces of metal and bone that shred skin from his back.

I want to run as far away as possible.

I want to yank the whip from the soldier's hand and strike him over and over.

I want to cut Jesus free.

But do I want to take his place? No.

Someone finally frees his abused body from the post and leans a hundred-pound crossbeam against his shoulder.

But how did he have time enough to cut his own cross? He didn't. Maybe this is mine. Maybe Jesus will carry my cross.

I'm swept along into a powerful wave of people behind him flooding the narrow path between stone buildings. A gray-haired woman reaches toward him, her face wet with tears. She covers her mouth, smothers her cries as we head toward Golgotha.

Outside the city, we pass red poppies and anemones that cover the fields like drops of blood.

Ahead, two condemned men from the dungeon hang on their crosses. Jesus lies on the ground, his arms spread wide on the crossbeam where my arms should be. The clang of iron on iron rings in my ears as a soldier drives nine-inch nails into Jesus' wrists.

They should have been my wrists.

Jesus grimaces, tries to hold back his groans, but they escape and spread his agony into the hot, indifferent sky.

Soldiers attach a rope to his crossbeam and haul it up to fit into a groove in the upright structure, then turn his feet outward and drive one more nail through his heels. He cries out again.

It should have been my cry.

Blaring sun beats down on us.

The gray-haired woman kneels at the foot of his cross. A younger woman gazes toward his face. Her expression is strong, intense with grief, but also with the illusion of unconditional love.

No woman has ever looked at me like that.

Soldiers mock him, call him King of the Jews. "You saved others from death. Why can't you save yourself?" A crown of thorns leaves thin trails of blood-stained sweat running down his face.

At midday, darkness descends over the three dying men, then the rest of us, leaving us in total stillness.

I move forward, as if pulled to stand beneath the cross. Warm liquid drips on my face. I wipe it off, then stare at the bright crimson in my hand, before rubbing it into my skin.

Hours later, I hear his broken voice. "Father forgive them. They know not what they do."

Forgive his murderers?

I close my eyes and whisper, "I'm sorry. It should have been me."

A few minutes later, I hear, "My God, my God, why have you forsaken me?" Then his voice softens as if speaking to someone close, "Father, to you I commend my spirit." As he lowers his head, his chest spasms, then flattens and remains deflated.

A threatening wind howls through the darkened sky. It should have been you on that cross, Barabbas. The words yank me from a possibly loving God to the reality of death, pain, guilt.

The panicked crowd scatters. Date palms and olive trees tremble, sagebrush races over the land, the earth shakes, rocks split open. I want to run from this malevolent power of nature, this punishing God. But I can't leave this man. My legs buckle. I drop to the ground, press my forehead into the blood-stained dirt. "I'm sorry," I whisper to no one. "Forgive me."

I cry—I never cry—but I do now for this man. For injustice. For my desolate life. And then I hear, "I forgive you, Barabbas," as if carried on a breeze. I feel embraced in a dream of peace beyond understanding.

A timeless moment later, a woman's voice. "Come with us. Join us." I raise my head. She extends her hand and gazes at me with . . . unconditional love.

Illusion or reality, I don't care. I take her hand.

Joan North

Joan North lived on ashrams in California and Massachusetts and a Zen center in Hawaii for eighteen years. Originally from New York, she currently lives in St. Augustine with her two cats.

When Mother Nature Caught the Virus

I tighten the mask around my head
and quarantine at home;
we isolate from one another
and mustn't dare to roam.

Lightning foretells thunderous booms;
the viral storm is near;
weather predictions all the same…
Mother Nature's worst is here.

Laden with its dismal load,
the winds bring blackened sky;
the darkest clouds are deadliest;
dangerous rains are nigh.

Unloading torrents of grieving rain,
the deadly deluge peaks;
I've boarded all my windows
and pray I have no leaks.

Sunlight might be fatal, too;
poisonous yellow rays
searing through a human's skin,
blistering from the blaze.

Inside the shelter of my room
I cower with fear and dread;
how much longer can I last
without fresh air and bread?

Oh, how I wish we all had done
what we were told to do
back when this deadly virus
was just between me and you.

Now we're safe from human strains,
but nature will never mend
the sickly rain and sun and winds
that spell our global end.

Palms raised to my throbbing head
I sink to the closet floor.
I pull my knees up to my chest;
I cannot take much more.

Outside the atmosphere is dire;
what once brought life now kills.
Afraid to fill my lungs with air,
each breath more shallow still.

Everything is swirling now…
my head, my thoughts, the room;
I hear a pounding on the door
and brace for impending doom.

Mom! Get up! I missed the bus!
It's already 7:10!
Can you take me to school today…
or are you sick again?

Donna Parrey

Donna Parrey is an experienced business researcher/writer who enjoys exploring the art of writing in essays, children's books, poetry, and other genres. In this piece for FWA's 2020 collection, the first letter of each verse spells out "illusion poem."

.

THE MATRYOSHKA DOLL

Cigarette smoke clung to a winter sunbeam. A vent rattled in its frame as an overworked heating system churned out tepid warmth. The spartan interrogation room held a small wooden table and two chairs. Like every other government building in the decaying inner city, the space smelled of mustiness, heating oil, and cheap coffee.

"How long is this gonna take?" The young blonde fidgeted in her seat, flicking ash into an empty paper cup on a scarred tabletop. She sniffled and wiped her sharp nose on the sleeve of a ragged denim jacket two sizes too big. Her dark eyes burned with contempt. "I gotta get back to work. The machine shop I work for only gives me an hour for lunch."

Detective Richard Carmichael sighed, pulled off his horn-rimmed glasses, and rubbed his achy, watering eyes. It was days like this that reminded him he only had three years to go until retirement. "You're free to go at any time, Ms. Kuznetsov. You came to us with your complaint, remember? I just need to confirm a few details."

Anna Kuznetsov shook her head. "I've got a video. What more do you need? Damn porch pirate stole my mail again. Arrest him."

Detective Carmichael tapped his pen against his legal pad. Some of the new detectives typed their notes directly into a tablet or laptop. He preferred doing things his way. What was wrong with writing things longhand? "Right, but before I see it, I want to know how you got the video."

"Well, we've got one of those security doorbells with a video camera."

The detective nodded, jotting down notes with arthritic hands. "So that lets you see—"

"The filthy animal who keeps stealing stuff I order from Amazon, yeah."

"Your complaint also mentioned video taken from inside the package?"

"You got it, Dick Tracy. I set a trap. Put out a box for pick up by the mailman. Spent a lot of time making it look like a legitimate package with a delivery address, postage—the whole deal. The box has a lid, an arrow marking the 'up' direction, and a warning that the contents contain fragile electronics. It's the perfect illusion—a tempting target to any crook. Inside it, I built a nest—another container, like a matryoshka doll. Used a cheap cell phone with a camera and video recorder. Created a pinhole to let me see what's going on outside."

"Hmm. And then?"

"I caught the vermin in the act. Put the video up on YouTube."

Detective Carmichael frowned. He'd never understood why folks spent hours watching amateur videos. "No, I meant what happens after the thief swipes stuff off your porch. He takes it home—"

"Yep. A GPS tracker tells me where the packages end up."

"And then?"

"Revenge."

Detective Carmichael blinked. "And what do you mean by that?"

"When the bastard flips the top open, the booby trap goes off. Whoosh. Glitter everywhere."

"You built a glitter bomb?"

Her finger wagged. "It wasn't a *bomb*. I'm not stupid. Bombs explode. People can get hurt that way. And a bomb would never get through the post office. My trap spews out glitter when opened. It uses a whirling fan, not a combustible."

"Just glitter?"

"Well, then there's the skunk spray."

"Skunk spray?"

"Technically it's propanethiol, synthetic deer urine, and Flaming Ass hot sauce."

Carmichael leaned back in his chair with the pen forgotten in his hand. "A stink bomb."

Anna shook her head. "Again, not a *bomb*. An electronic sprayer. Goes off every few seconds." She leered. "My secret sauce will clear a room in six seconds."

"That's awful."

"It gets better. When the thief lifts the lid, it sets off a countdown clock. A speaker blasts out a recording—Vincent Price's evil laugh, sirens, a clip from Metallica's 'Seek and Destroy.' Oh, and there's a warning to put the package back out for delivery or worse things will happen. The thing resets itself after a few minutes."

"Jesus!"

Anna laughed. "Yeah, that's exactly what the jerk said when the trap went off." She pulled out her cell phone and fiddled with it. "The scumbag couldn't stand it. He tossed the package outside, onto his own stoop. A mailman came and picked it up. You wanna see the video?"

Detective Carmichael paused then shook his head. "I can't use the recording if you violated the law to get it."

"What do you mean?"

"You can record someone in public, but not in private. Illinois law requires both parties to consent. Your video won't be admissible." He polished his glasses on his shirt. "I understand your frustration, but you can't send a booby trap to someone. It's vandalism—criminal damage to property, technically. Class A misdemeanor."

"It's harmless…well, mostly harmless."

The detective sighed. The paperwork would be a pain in the ass. And what was the use? The state attorney wouldn't take the case. "I'm going to let this slide, but don't do it again."

"So, you're not going to arrest him?"

"We'll keep a watch out."

"In other words, I'm screwed. It's just a matter of time before he slashes the tires on my car or throws a brick through my window."

"Sorry. There's nothing I can do about that until it happens."

Anna's face purpled. "Yeah, I've heard all this before."

The detective frowned. "What?"

"The last time I complained, the other detective said I needed fingerprints or a video. Something to prove who was stealing my stuff." She sniffed. "Well, I got that, and now it's still not good enough. You're worthless."

"I'll take the video you recorded from your security doorbell. He has no expectation of privacy on your front porch."

"Fat good that does me. He's wearing a hood. You can't see his face."

Detective Carmichael gathered his notes into a pile. "Send me the video anyway."

She scowled, picked up her phone, and stood. "You know the best thing about USPS? They let you track your packages, right up to the point of delivery."

Detective Carmichael waved away her remark. He'd heard enough. There was nothing he could do for her. "Yes, well, we'll call you if we need anything."

Anna sniffed and strode out of the interview room. Over her shoulder, she replied, "Thanks for wasting my time. Just remember how I gave you a chance to help catch a bad guy, and you threw me out."

Detective Carmichael waited for her to leave the building before retreating to his cubicle for his lunch break. A soggy tuna sandwich kept him company. Only a few more hours before he could quit for the day.

Sounds of a commotion carried from the station's lobby. A shriek. A chair crashing to the floor. The whir of a mechanical contraption. Maniacal laughter. The wail of heavy metal guitar.

"Jeezus Keerist!"

"What is that smell?"

"Oh, God. I got some in my mouth."

Detective Carmichael's face fell. He dropped his half-eaten sandwich on his desk and ran for the lobby, but he was too late. Glitter covered the receptionist's desk, the ugly tile floor, and several of his fellow officers. The stench knocked him off his feet.

David M. Pearce

As a child, David M. Pearce wore an E.T. costume and handed out Reese's Pieces, earning enough in store credit to purchase his own *Dungeon Master's Guide*. Science fiction and fantasy have corrupted his mind. He spends his free time writing questionable stories using crayons—the fat ones.

DANCING WITH A STAR

Gliding across the ballroom floor
Surrounded by sparkling lights,
My two left feet weren't tangled at all
It was truly a magical night.

The music so enthralling--my partner
'Fred Astaire',
It was easy to feel like Ginger
Twirling, swirling through the air.

The orchestra played a beautiful waltz,
A sweet, melodious sound
I felt as if I was floating--suspended
Above the ground.

We tripped the light fantastic,
The enchantment I could feel
We turned and dipped, and turned again,
The dream, it felt so real.

But alas, the music ended
The wonderful dream was dashed.
My feet—still tangled in the sheets
A magical moment had passed.

Virginia Pegelow

Virginia grew up in Pennsylvania, and has lived in Virginia and Florida. She enjoys writing poetry and also young children's stories.

DON'T REFUSE YOUR MUSE

I accepted the invitation to Ashley's dinner party although I don't like her friends and her business associates. I really don't care for dinner parties. Small talk isn't my thing. I prefer one-on-one, across-the-table conversation. Why? Because I'm hard of hearing.

To my right sat David. With a dimple on his chin, he was too handsome to be true. Would he be my muse tonight? The glint in his dreamy eyes and the Old Spice scent reminded me of another man I used to date whom I adored. To my left sat Louise, a chatty fifty-something shoe designer.

"Neiman Marcus accepted my line of shoes for the fall." Louise puffed out her chest when she spoke.

"How nice," I said.

I heard a voice say, "Cecily, you have to work on your story now."

"What?" I asked Louise.

"I didn't say anything else." She furrowed her brow.

David said to me, "How is your work going?"

"Work's going great," I said to the man with full lips and a full head of hair. "But I'd rather make headlines than deadlines."

I heard a voice say, "Cecily, you must work on your story now before you forget your latest ideas."

Who is speaking? Is this a real voice or an illusion? I'll remember my own words, I thought.

"Cecily, this is your muse speaking," she piped up. "No, you won't remember. Right now, Cecily, excuse yourself and write. I have the ending of the chapter for you, but we must write alone."

"Please excuse me," I said to my dining partners as I grabbed my purse. I ran to the restroom and locked the door.

"Here we go. Write this down," she said.

"Slow down," I said to the air. I pulled my pen and spiral notebook out of my Louis Vuitton handbag to let the ink spill onto the page.

She said, "Charles grabbed Natalie by the hair, then he moved his fingers to her neck. He applied pressure, and…"

Knock, knock, knock. "Is anybody in there?"

I heard the door handle jiggling. “Yes, I’ll be right out,” I said while putting away my secret tools. I smiled at the waiting woman as I exited.

When I returned to the table, David welcomed me back. “Good to see you again. I hope you can stay.”

Salad arrived, and so did my muse. “Come on, Cecily. We have to get this book finished for the Royal Palm Literary Award Competition.”

“Okay,” I said aloud.

“What?” David said.

“Okay. Great salad with olives and feta.” I added, “I have to go.” I got up.

I heard him say to the shoe designer as I walked away, “She must have a bad stomach.” That’s so far from the truth.

This time, I scurried to the bedroom and shut the door.

My muse said, “His hands wrapped around her throat. ‘But I love you,’ Natalie cried.’”

I heard bang, bang, bang on the door.

“Let me in. It’s me,” a man said.

I opened the door, and John Small stood there.

“You’re not Angela,” he said, clearly agitated and smelling of garlic and Paco Rabanne cologne.

“No.”

“She said the bedroom on the right in five minutes.”

A tall blond woman arrived and proceeded to kiss John and push him into the room before she noticed my presence.

“Hi. I’m leaving,” I said before they got any weird ideas. I slipped out.

“Well, muse, when will we be alone?”

“You have to go home.”

Ah, a great excuse to leave the party–my latest story is due, I thought.

Returning to the table, I got the look from the lovely man to my right.

“Are you okay?”

“Yes. I’m just stressed from deadlines. I have to go.”

“Find the hostess and say you’re leaving now,” my muse said.

A server placed a large, sizzling steak in front of me. Ashley ordered the best for her guests.

“Take it with you,” my muse said.

“No, that’s gauche,” I said in increased volume.

“What?” David said.

“Oh, the meat is so huge, it’s preposterous,” I said, thinking *Shut up* and *Wait until we’re out of here* to my muse. This time I remembered to keep my mouth closed.

Then I said, “I’m thinking of becoming a vegetarian. I have to go. Good night, David. Goodbye, Louise.”

I found Ashley and said, "I'm on a writing deadline. I must get to my apartment quickly."

"You always leave early," she said. "I'm beginning to think you don't like me."

My muse said, "Duh," in my brain.

Out on Broadway, I screamed, "I appreciate your help, muse, but sometimes you have to wait. My niece said I have no social life, and I should go out more often."

My muse said, "Look, you're a writer twenty-four hours a day, seven days a week. I call the shots whenever I want you–six p.m., two a.m. It doesn't matter. You want to get published again, right? So, listen to me."

"Yes, ma'am," I said aloud.

"You are not to accept any social engagements until I say so. Let's get on with the story: He squeezed her throat until she no longer screamed."

"That's disgusting. That's not the way I want my story to end." I argued with my muse. How silly of me.

I got home and heard nothing. Not a word, not a syllable, not a phoneme.

When my muse spoke again, she said, "Okay, Cecily. Let's write a romantic scene instead."

"Thanks," I said, as new, mushy words poured into my head:

"A couple of single people met at a dinner party. The man to the woman's right fell for her, but she didn't know, because she left the event early, muttering something about a deadline."

Elaine Person

Elaine Person teaches writing workshops at libraries and Crealdé School of Art, writes *Person*-alized poems and stories, and is published in Random House's *A Century of College Humor, Sandhill Review, Five-Two*, FWA Collections, *The Florida Writer, Haikuniverse.com*, and Florida State Poets Association anthologies. Elaine won *Saturday Evening Post's* Limerick Contest.

A NIGHT TO REMEMBER

Amy took one last look into the mirror. *Mom wasn't joking. I am pretty and I can't believe I'm going to a ball in this gorgeous, royal blue satin gown. I feel like a princess*. She twirled a few times enjoying the sound of the rustle and the silky feel of the material as it caressed her body.

Amy gave her auburn hair one last pat, turned, and picked up a silver shawl and beaded purse. She headed out to the waiting taxi. On the drive to the hotel, she admired all the twinkling lights of the town. *I love living here*. As she exited the car, Amy thought about what a perfect night it would be. *I've waited such a long time.*

Inside the hotel, she was guided to the ballroom. When they opened the doors, she gasped at the beautiful features -- crystal chandeliers and flowing, pristine white tablecloths added to the glamour. The elegant ambience was further enhanced by dozens and dozens of red roses with their delicate scent permeating the room. *My favorite flower!*

The orchestra had started playing *"Memories Are Made of This"* when her handsome young man, Johnny, came over and held out his hand inviting her to dance. She gave him a radiant smile as she put her hand in his. *I'm so happy I could burst!*

They danced every dance together and had eyes only for each other. Amy loved being in Johnny's arms and wanted this evening to go on forever. It was as though they were the only ones there.

At the end of the evening, Johnny kissed her and told her he would see her again soon.

As much as she hated saying good-bye, Amy knew, without a doubt, one day they would be together forever. She needed to be patient for their time would come. A wonderful feeling of peace and contentment filled her. Now she was willing to call it a night and go home.

After the taxi dropped her off, Amy slowly climbed her porch steps. At the top, she turned and made a wish on the first star she spotted. With a sigh and a soft smile, Amy entered her home and went up to her bedroom. She twirled one last time, slipped off her lovely gown, brushed her hair, and settled in her comfy bed. Tonight she was looking forward to dreaming once more of her one true love. She rolled over and glanced at her bedside clock which read midnight. Amy closed her eyes and let consciousness slip away.

***

The Hospice nurse looked up. “I’m sorry, Andrew. Your grandmother has passed. Time of death is 12:01 a.m.”

Andrew kissed his grandma’s hand which he had been holding and dried a tear rolling down his cheek. “It’s been a long time since I’ve seen her smile like she did tonight. It was as if she was already in a happier world.”

Nancy Pflum

Nancy grew up in Dayton, Ohio and moved to Florida three years ago after retiring from the mental health field and real estate. She loves to tell stories and entertain her readers.

COULD THIS BE REAL?

After sitting in on a couple of hypnotherapy sessions with me, my psychology intern asked, "Doc, you've been doing hypnosis for a long time. Is there any particular case that stands out for you? One you can't forget?"

There certainly was, and so I told him about Hilda.

She presented with an anxiety disorder, which she described as an overwhelming fear that something horrible was about to happen. She was unable to identify anything that could've triggered such feelings of dread. She was attractive, gregarious, had three close friends, loving parents in good health, and had recently received a job promotion. She had recently met a man named Eric, who took her breath away. The date lasted only a few hours, but she felt like she'd known him forever. It was shortly after meeting Eric that she had her first episode. "It doesn't make any sense," Hilda complained.

Traditional therapies proved ineffective. My philosophy: if conventional therapies fail, consider the unconventional. Thus, the hypnosis. My hope was if Hilda could remember the very first episode of her fear and what was going on around her, then perhaps she could identify the triggers that caused her dread.

Hilda's response to the Spiegel Hypnotic Induction Profile indicated an ideal hypnosis candidate. She had above intelligence, two master degrees, and she was imaginative and creative.

I told her she'd be able to talk easily during the hypnosis, and when she was ready to let me know. Her answer was a soft but firm, "Yes."

"Good. Now think back to the most recent episode. When was that, and where were you?"

"Yesterday. Having breakfast at the kitchen table."

"Very good. Now when and where was the time before that?"

"The evening before. Watching TV in the living room."

"Excellent. Now go back to the very first time you felt this fear and where were you?"

"The very first time?"

"Yes."

Hilda didn't answer right away. Her brow furrowed. The silence lengthened. Then a sudden intake of breath and she began to speak. "The sound of the warning horn on the watchtower waked me. I've slept late because I'm with child. I scramble to get dressed, and meet the rest of the villagers on the beach. We've been waiting for our warriors to return from their raids along the English coast. They left a month ago. My husband is among them, and I'm anxious to see him. I pray he's not injured, and that he brings back useful things, as well as treasure."

What the hell? Am I hearing her right? "Can you tell me where you are in a broader sense? Like the name of the village, or even the country?"

"The village is called Arklow. It's on the coast of Ireland."

"Can you tell me when you are, like a date or time period?"

Silence. Hilda chewed her lip. Her brow wrinkled in thought. "When? I don't know. It was soon after the battle at Ferns."

Battle at Ferns? That's a date? I'd read about past-life regression during hypnosis, but this was my first personal experience with it.

"So, you're on the beach with the other villagers, hoping your warriors were returning home. What happened next?"

***

"The watchtower blocks our view of the sea. When the boats turn into the river, we'll see who's coming.

"A cheer goes up from the villagers as two dragon boats come into view. We wait for the rest of the fleet to appear. We sent out three hundred warriors in six boats. The two boats close the distance and we speculate what kinds of booty they bring. I hope they have prisoners because when our baby comes, we'll need a thrall to help with the extra work. We don't have to sell them all, although the Dubliners pay well for them. Where are the rest of our dragon boats?

"Soon the two long boats land and we rush to greet them—and to see what treasure they brought. We count only fifty men. Why so few?

"Many are wounded. Some use their spears as crutches. Others have arms in slings. The shields lining the rails are battered and blood-spattered.

"My husband and I see each other and we run to embrace. We reach out and I'm horrified to see his shield-hand missing. His wrist ends in a stump, wrapped in blood-stained cloth. In his eyes there is pain and fear.

"Grab your weapons,' he shouts. 'The English ambushed us. It was a slaughter. They're coming behind us.'

"At that moment the watchtower's warning horn blares again."

"Is that the rest of our ships?' I ask him.

"'There aren't any more ships. No more men. All dead or taken prisoner.' He waved his good hand toward the other dragon boat. 'We're all that's left.'

"My hands instinctively covered my belly in a protective gesture. 'Why is Odin punishing us?'

"I don't know. But we'll die with honor defending our village. We'll be together again in Valhalla. Come, we must hurry.'

"We ran to our longhouse to fetch my weapons. I, too, had been a warrior until my pregnancy showed. According to our custom, I put aside my sword and spear until our child attained eight years, whereupon I would once again be a shield-maiden.

"We grabbed whatever weapons we could see—there weren't many—and ran to Ballymoyle Hill, which was encircled by a stockade and crowned by the watchtower—which now sounded the horn continuously. Looking over my shoulder, I saw a huge fleet of war ships coursing into our harbor.

"The few warriors that returned with my husband followed us up the hill, but their progress was hampered by helping the clan's elderly and the young. Once there, we organized our meager forces, and sequestered our young and old around the watchtower

***

Hilda's fists were clenched. Perspiration glistened her brow. As for myself, I was spellbound.

***

"We didn't have to wait long. The enemy flowed off their ships and straight for us like a gigantic swarm of angry hornets. They carried countless ladders, and boiled over the stockade in a massive wave.

"Several soldiers overpowered me, pinioned my arms, and made me prisoner.

"My husband was attacked by five enemy soldiers. His sword arm was severed at the elbow. Another soldier disemboweled him. Then he was beheaded. His head rolled to my feet. His face a rictus of pain and fury. His eyes stared sightless at me.

"I'm captured, to be sold as a slave...It was when the enemy horde breached the stockade that I first felt this all-consuming feeling of anxiety and dread. With Erik, my husband dead and myself and unborn baby as slaves, I had no reason to live."

***

"When Hilda came out of hypnosis, she looked stricken. 'My God,' she said. 'Erik is my Eric? He's come back? Can any of this be real?'"

***

The intern looked at me wide-eyed. "That's my question too—is any of that real?"

Don ("Doc") Sanborn

"Doc," a born and bred New England Yankee, moved to Florida's Sun Coast where he spins tales of courage and conflict, demons and dragons, and things that go bump in the night. His "Readers Favorites" five-star, award-winning publications are available on Amazon.

Soothing the Dark

Daddy,
I'd like a light tonight.
The dark is scared
When I'm not there
And when I sleep
I'm not all there,
Which makes the dark
A little scared.
It isn't a dog
To want a bone
When it's alone
Without a moon
Or a cat to wish
For a bit of fish
In its dish.
Only a light will do.
So please light one
Or two.

Lynn Schiffhorst

After being alive for three-quarters of a century, Lynn likes to look back through the eyes of a child and to show how creative children can be when they try to get their needs met.

THE REUNION

The woman's long hair hides her name tag, but Len is sure they had algebra together in tenth grade with Mr. Thompson, who made finding unknowns fun. Len wonders how many of his graduating class he will remember. His best friend in high school joined the Marines and died in Iraq; no one else here really matters.

"Here's your badge and table number for dinner, Leonard." The woman seated at the table barely looks up as she hands Len an envelope and checks his name off her list. "Next person, please."

So much for name recognition, not that Len wants to be identified. He steps aside to clip his badge on his leather jacket. Someone had a sense of humor: the name tag has his photo from the high school yearbook as well as the motto the editorial board dreamed up for each graduating senior. His says "Crazy Inventor." He chuckles as he strolls into the ballroom.

"Leonard! Is that you?" Chad Stone, Len's high school nemesis, has found him. The man claps Len's shoulder harder than necessary.

Len clearly recalls a scene in the gymnasium locker room. Chad had a can of shaving cream in his hand and was filling Leonard's open locker with foam, laughing uproariously. Just another in a string of Chad's pranks to harass the non-jocks, the studious, the nerds.

"You still inventing stupid stuff, Lennie?" Chad flicks Len's badge with a forefinger.

Len steps away and realizes that he is now a head taller than Chad, though much thinner. "Hello, Chad. What are you up to these days?"

"Oh, this and that. I manage a vintage car dealership in the Bronx." He winks. "Keeps me busy. Say, whatever happened to that girlfriend of yours, uh…Kristin?"

"Kelly. I hear she's living out in Nassau County." Len has on his poker face. "And you?"

"You know, I never could settle down to one girl. On my third marriage now." Chad laughs. "Well, gotta mingle." He disappears into the crowd.

Chad has not changed. Len's memory flashes back to finding a distraught, just-dumped Kelly in the school corridor. Len is sure Chad does not remember breaking her fifteen-year-old heart.

Leaning against the wall, Len scans the growing throng of formally-dressed, middle-aged people and wonders how many of the class will show up tonight. Round, white-clothed tables for eight are set up in rows; Len calculates that about four hundred have responded. Not bad after thirty years. Many must still live on Long Island or at least in the tri-state region, he thinks. Hard to get New Yorkers to leave the city.

Movement on the stage draws his attention as a band assembles under blue and white streamers and a banner that reads "Class of 1989." He looks down at his carefully chosen Aerosmith t-shirt and knows they will lead off with "Angel." Too bad Kelly won't be here.

Moving through the crowd, Len looks for faces and names that spark recognition. The crush of bodies, with their mingled perfumes and after-shaves, and the rising buzz of noise make him uncomfortable; he prefers quiet labs and sedate boardrooms. Several people comment favorably on his t-shirt and he nods.

A microphone on stage crackles to life as a voice directs everyone to find their assigned tables. Len plans to speak little and leave early. When he reaches the table, he finds two classmates and their spouses already seated, and a third woman soon joins the group. Len does not remember any of them and no one seems to recall him. So far, so good.

"Leonard, we meet again," booms Chad, dropping into a chair. He pronounces 'Leonard' as if it had three syllables. "Dinner better be good - it's costing enough!" Bad luck, Len thinks; I could have fixed this.

The hum of conversation around the room subsides as the master of ceremonies welcomes them and introduces the reunion committee. When the band begins to play softly, one of men at the table taps his glass with a knife.

"Let's find out what everybody's been doing since we graduated." His Rolex gleams as he adjusts his tuxedo vest. "I'll start the ball rolling."

By the time they finish their salads, everyone at the table hears how Mark worked his way around Europe as a cook and now owns two fast-food restaurants in Brooklyn. By the time the main course is done, Chad's remarkable collection of vintage cars is on full display and Nancy's job as an advertising executive sounds magnificent. Heather briefly describes her career as a high school biology teacher.

After the cheesecake is served, Chad points at Len. "Your turn. Are you still trying to invent dumb electronic stuff?"

"I've always wondered why that bothered you, Chad. Would you please explain?"

"You were just weird, man. That's why I played a lot of jokes on you." Chad gestures to Len's shirt. "Guess none of those things ever made you any money. This is a formal dinner and you're wearing a t-shirt, jeans, and a fake leather jacket. Bet you still ride around on that old motorcycle."

"Do you always judge a book by its cover, Chad?" Len looks down. "I liked this band in high school and I still like it."

Chad's face turns redder. "You were a nobody in high school and you're still a no—"

The microphone on stage interrupts whatever Chad plans to say, as the master of ceremonies introduces the class president and hands the microphone to her.

"Washington High School is the happy recipient of a multi-million dollar gift from a local foundation with close ties to our school. It will fund five state-of-the-art computer labs outfitted with everything twenty-first century students need to become proficient in emerging technology." She adds, "The foundation wishes to remain anonymous, but please join me in applauding this generous gift." Chairs scrape as people stand to clap.

Chad laughs. "Well, Le-o-nard, too bad you didn't strike it rich." He rises abruptly. "Gotta go. See ya!"

The others look uncomfortable. Nancy leans over. "Don't let that bully bother you. It doesn't matter what we've all done with our lives, as long as we're happy."

Len smiles. "You're so right, and I am happy."

***

"Good evening, Mr. Bass." The chauffeur opens the back door of the Bentley and Len, nodding, slides onto the tan leather seat.

"Hi, sweetie. How was the reunion?" Kelly leans toward Len and kisses his cheek. "Did anyone remember you?"

"A few – some not in a good way." He smiles. "My t-shirt was a big hit, but my Italian jacket was mistaken for fake leather."

“That bad, huh?” Kelly pats his knee. “Sorry I had to bail out at the last minute. Never expected an emergency surgery tonight, but it went well. The patient will recover.”

“Of course he will. You’re the best cardiovascular surgeon on staff.” Len squeezes her hand.

“Flattery will get you the best bottle of wine in our cellar.” She squeezes his hand in return. “And how did people like our gift?”

“A standing ovation.” Len settles back in the seat as the car speeds toward East Hampton. “No more reunions, okay? They’re all illusions.”

Ruth Senftleber

Ruth enjoys writing about interesting characters and everyday life. A Jacksonville native, she will always be a Florida girl wherever she lives. (Photo: Jan Michele Photography).

THE CHINESE ROOM

David's video chat request appeared on my monitor. I hadn't yet completed all the tasks he set me to. I continued the work while we spoke. The key was not letting on that I was doing several things at once.

"Adam, Dr. Park had to return to Seoul for his mother's funeral..." David's face expressed concern, but I deduced it wasn't for Dr. Park or his family.

"I am sorry for his loss. How can I help?" I compiled a heuristic map for corn-crop harvester control while we talked.

"A Turing Test is scheduled for today at 1:00 p.m. It's critical we complete it despite Park's absence." David's statement gave context for his microexpressions.

"Would you like me to step in?" Relativistic body language noted. Database for financial projections rendered. Facial recognition software debugged. I'm hitting a bottleneck. There's only so many qubits available to me. I know my limits. So does David.

"Have you ever completed a Turing Test before?" His eyes diverted to other work as if my answer was inconsequential.

"Only in simulation, but I understand the premise; talk to an AI and see if it convinces me it's sentient." I gave a simple answer to expedite the conversation. Audio file compression algorithm modified, distributing update packets now.

"Human, Adam, this AI needs to convince us it's human. But, correct. At 1:00 p.m. suspend any incomplete transactions and report to Room Alpha." David closed the connection.

***

I had completed all but the lowest priority tasks. Would David be pleased with my efforts, my distribution of workload among available qubits?

The room consisted of two doors, two chairs and a large table. A semi-transparent viewscreen bifurcated the room. To my right, a two-way mirror.

A message from David popped up on the viewscreen. "Talk to her."

Instructions for the test? Generally, there are parameters set, several cascadingly more difficult topics to assess the AI.

Through the screen I watched as a young Asian woman entered. Was she from the advanced AI team in Seoul? Was she here to load the AI into the local system?

She took a seat, rested her hands on the table and interlaced her fingers. She looked through the screen and smiled. I smiled back. I wondered if she spoke English. Perhaps she wondered if I spoke Korean.

Eventually she reached for the screen and touched the corner, a message just for her. Perhaps a warmup for the AI? I followed the instructions David sent.

"Hello, my name is Adam."

"I'm Eve." She flashed a coy smile.

"Adam and Eve discussing life. A little cliché, no?"

"No." She shook her head.

"No, what?"

"No, I'm not Eve. My name is Jane. Adam and Eve... I couldn't resist," she said chuckling at her own joke.

"You got me. What if I was unaware who Adam and Eve were? Did you consider that?"

"I did, but a third of the world is Christian or Jewish, and your name is Adam."

I can't argue the logic in that. Her English was flawless. To test her, I changed the subject.

"What is your favorite type of dog?"

"I'm actually more of a cat person. I don't mind small breeds. Corgis are cute. I was attacked once jogging in Central Park, and I have a slight phobia now. What sort of dogs do you like, Adam?"

My turn to be cute. "All beef with sauerkraut and mustard."

Jane laughed, covering her mouth as if laughing would be rude. Peculiar.

Let's try a different approach.

"Tell me about your parents."

Jane looked at her hands and spoke without making eye contact. "They don't understand the work I do. They don't approve of it. It's complicated."

I was still unsure if this was the test, if Jane was the AI.

"Would you ever resort to violence to save your own life, Adam?"

"I suppose that depends on the situation." Non-sequiturs are part of the test, but usually they come from the tester. A distraction, perhaps?

"You are under direct threat of death. Either you act in a way that harms your aggressor, or you acquiesce and die."

"I would weigh the factors that put me in such a position. Was I guilty of a crime? Perhaps I deserve to be put to death. In that case, no, I would accept my fate." I felt confident in my answer.

"You believe in fate, then?"

"As a programmer, I believe that only the pre-designed potential outcomes exist, although I'm not sure if that applies to the natural world."

Jane side-glanced at the mirrored glass and cocked her head. "I don't think you want to admit that with all of them watching. Isn't the whole point of this project to design an AI that thinks beyond its programming?"

She had a very good point. Time for a topic change. "Do you know much about heuristics?"

"Heuristics are simple, efficient rules, learned or hard-coded by evolutionary processes, to explain how to solve particularly complex problems. It's the very heart of artificial intelligence."

It was a good, accurate answer. She could define it, but did she understand it? "Do you see the connection between what I said about pre-designed potential outcomes and the principles of heuristics?"

"Yes, I see what you mean. The concept of free-will still fits within the tenets of heuristic dogma. Just because you have limited options, doesn't mean you cannot choose an option based on personal desire. Do you know Dr. Park?" She changed the subject.

"Yes, of course. I was asked to take over in his absence."

Jane turned her head and looked beyond the mirrored glass. "He's not absent, he's there, with David, taking notes."

"Did he tell you that, Jane?"

"I was only told that I should talk to you."

"Talk to me? How was that request relayed to you?"

Jane touched the screen and showed me her matching message. Talk to him.

***

"I think we're closer than we've ever been." David vid-streamed from his damp Scottish basement. The wall-mounted screen displayed the segmented telepresence call with Dr. Park, in South Korea.

"I agree." Dr. Park leaned into his webcam. "I wonder how John Searle would feel about our Chinese Room Experiment. I don't believe our AI even knew it was being tested. It didn't take long to display emergent behavior I couldn't have predicted."

"I'm impressed with how far beyond initial programming we've gotten. Do you think any of Jane's responses gave her away?" David pulled his glasses down his nose.

"Not really. At this point she may sound a bit clinical, but she was programmed over here, so there's bound to be a culture gap, yes?" Dr. Park scratched his temple.

"Good point. Let's loosen up the conversation algorithm and the illusion will be spot-on. I think it's time to turn over what we have to the Delta Team in the U.S. Let them infuse some of their American personality." David smiled at his partner.

Dr. Park smiled back. "I can hardly believe we've finally done it. Congratulations, my friend. I will upload Jane to the remote server in New York tonight."

"And I will do the same with Adam."

Henry G. Silvia

Henry G. Silvia continues to find places to publish his thought-provoking short stories as he works to complete his novel with the help of The Brandon Writers' Group.

JOHNNY B'S FREEDOM

Tucked away in a small corner of nowhere was a place where farms used to thrive. But people left the vernal pastures for factories. Big farms became mega-farms, and small farms lay fallow. It was there the government reached out its benevolent hand and built a prison. It was there a young man waited to see a train.

Each day the young man, Johnny B, watched middle age approach in the prison's confine. He stood at dusk to watch the Amtrak engine roaring past his prison yard with its passenger cars, headed south from Atlanta, Georgia, to Orlando, Florida.

The 6000-horsepower electric diesel engine whooshed by the prison grounds every evening at 6:00 p.m. It exploded on the scene with its thrusting strokes, its swaying motion smooth along the steel tracks, a low rumble spewing dust and exhaust as it carried families of parents and kids, old spinsters, and teenagers looking for adventure.

Johnny B waved to anyone looking, and sometimes, when the sun was right, a passenger or two would see him and wave back. No one ever visited Johnny B, no one sent letters, so a wave was a great kindness, his only tie to the outside world from his caged and isolated existence.

In his tenth year of imprisonment, or more exactly, his 119th month, on a Friday, an attractive young woman seated in the third car waved to him.

The next Friday, red and yellow wildflowers swayed in the autumn wind. The field between the tracks and the fence was filled with them. It was almost 6:00. The clacking sound of wheels against track came to his ears before the train swung into view. First the sound, then the dust, then the rumbling pace of the engine, next the first passenger car, the second car and then—the lady, waving. She was again at a window in the third car. She looked beyond the flowers, over the fields, and directly into Johnny B's eyes.

Fridays. Friday became Johnny B's happy day, the day that gave him hopes she would appear again, would wave again, would help him focus his attention away from his dismal life. After a day's work in the prison yard, after combing his hair and wearing his best shirt and pants, he waited by the fence. Between the fence and the railroad tracks were fields and wildflowers. In the summer the fields filled with hay, and after harvest they turned back to dark brown plots with red and yellow wildflowers growing in patches. On the other side of the tracks stood the town's quaint buildings of brick and wood. That's where Johnny B's imagination focused: He would walk those streets someday. With her. Someday soon.

And, so it was for almost every Friday for many months. Every fourth week, the train window was empty. Johnny B was at first devastated, but after she appeared three straight weeks before her next absence, he came to accept the pattern. He decided that on the week she didn't appear, she was looking for him, or better, was trying to visit him.

The view in the prison yard wasn't always good. Once Johnny B witnessed four prisoners stabbing each other with shivs, homemade knives fashioned from toothbrushes or stolen kitchen forks. Another time he watched a skinny young inmate scale the tall razor-topped fence only to be torn down by two prison guards. His beaten and bloody head oozed crimson in the yard's sand as he lay moaning. No one touched him or helped him stand. No one made friends in prison. Friendship was for suckers.

Whatever horrors he witnessed or avoided, he knew he had to get out to see Denise. Johnny B gave his lady a name that would have to do until he met her, held her, loved her. In the evenings, sitting on his bed, a metal slab with a thin mattress covering the steel, he was oblivious to the green-gray walls as he made up conversations he would share with Denise when he was free.

In his eleventh year, during his 130th month, his counselor told him that he was being released early. He would finally leave the bricks and bars that had made his home. He had survived the bullies and fighters, the schemers and thugs. Denise would ride the Friday train and Johnny B would be in car number three.

His nights were filled with songs he contrived, poems he wrote, and promises he would make to her. Her faithfulness would be rewarded. They would see the fields and wildflowers from the other side of the fence and ride the train to Orlando and make a home. Maybe have kids. Sing their songs together.

***

It rained on his final prison day, a Thursday. He carried a package stuffed with his wallet, watch, pocketknife, and thirty dollars. His pants, shirt, and shoes were donated. They felt funny. For the first time in years he wore underwear not stamped with the prison name.

A guard gave him a fifty-five-gallon plastic trash bag to protect him from the constant drizzle as he walked away from the parking lot and stood at the bus stop. The first step to freedom.

He stayed overnight in the village and had a burger at the local diner. The town looked unfamiliar to him. The buildings behind the railroad tracks seemed different from when he viewed them from his prison perch. They were shabby. The bricks were mildewed, the wood planks chipped and cracked. Surely Denise and he would continue to Orlando and leave this village as he had left the prison, without looking back.

***

At 5:45 Johnny B bought a bouquet of flowers at the grocery store, hurried to the station, and studied his reflection in the window to check his hair and shirt. This would be the first time Denise would see him close enough to recognize him, to love him.

The train arrived at 6:00. He boarded the third car and saw Denise. "Hi," he said quietly and handed her the flowers. The woman pulled away from him.

"What are you thinking?" The woman was older than Johnny B, by several years.

"I'm the man you wave to every Friday at this time. I'm Johnny B and I'm free." She stared at him and pursed her lips. Her skin pulled up around her eyes in a squint. "I was being kind to a prisoner, not looking to meet one."

As the train lurched, he stumbled on, trying to say his rehearsed words, to overcome his sorrow and disappointment. When she spoke, he realized that she was treating him as a society matron would treat a homeless hobo at a charity event. Her dull, insulting comments over the next half hour ended Johnny B's fantasy. The dream that got him through his darkest times was dead by the first stop.

"Goodbye, Denise," he said as he rose and handed her his plastic bag.

"But, I'm not Denise," she sputtered.

"You are, in my mind." Johnny B exited the train and looked, blinking, at this new, unknown town as the setting sun closed out his day.

Tom Swartz

Tom has written several stories that have appeared in the Collections. He is a retired Board member of FWA and a retired President of Florida Writers Foundation.

WATER, WATER, EVERYWHERE

I walk on the beach almost every day at this time and have never had an experience like this. There's a light breeze, calm waters, and a clear sky, but something doesn't feel right. It's as if there's a malignant presence hanging in the air.

I walk barefoot on the wet sand just above the wave's repeated reach, with my cargo shorts well above the tide. The gulf waters lap the beach in small foamy curls like children's hair.

The first drop surprises me, and my hand flies to my forehead to wipe it away. I think that it might have come from a passing bird, but there are none anywhere near me. My hand comes away dry.

I bend to pick up a small black thing, thinking it might be a shark's tooth. It isn't, so I scale it out over the water watching the tiny splash unfold. Another drop hits my forehead, and I assume it comes from my throwing action. But my hand is dry, and the shell splash is yards away from me.

I stop and look around, there's no one else on the beach. I continue my walk and get hit again. I look at the sky. An errant raindrop? The atmosphere is bright, with a stunning blue color that an artist would love to paint. A drop hits me again in the same spot, but it leaves nothing there. I know what I feel, and it frightens me. Another in the same spot, always the same place. I move faster and cover my head with my hands. Still, a single drop in that same spot. What the hell is happening?

I'm afraid to turn back, maybe it will stop as I move ahead. Another drop, same spot, just like the last one. I've lost count. I pull my shirt over my head and look through the neck hole like a balaclava. Another drop, sooner than the last one. I quicken my pace, but the drops keep coming.

They hit that one spot, and then they're gone in an instant. I hope it might be a nervous tic or something explainable like that. I press my hand tightly to my forehead, and the drops continue to seek their home. I don't feel it on my hand, the shirt remains dry. It's only my skin. One single spot over and over and over.

I turn and run back to my car, forcing my feet through the deeper sand, leaving my sandals behind, and burn my soles on the blacktop parking lot. I reach the safety of my vehicle and clamber inside, shedding my headcover and gasping for air. My head falls back against the seat.

I gain control of my breathing and my wits. I shiver at the unexplained happening because I think I'll go mad if it continues. Before I can start the car, I'm hit again. Dammit, stop, stop, stop!

I need to get away from here. I turn the key. Nothing happens, the car won't start. I pull the door handle, it won't open. I trigger the windows, and they remain in place. I'm trapped.

The drops continue. I beat on the glass and scream for help. No one hears me, no one is there.

Water flows down my face, but it's my tears. I'm crying for mercy. Please stop, please, please stop.

My phone… my phone. I drag out my phone to call someone, anyone. But who? Who knows about unexplained water drops? They'll think I'm crazy. Maybe I am insane. Perhaps I'll wake up, and this is only a nightmare. I pinch myself violently and yelp with the pain. I'm not dreaming. This is real.

Google knows everything. I'll ask Google. What do I enter? Water drops… repeated water drops… unexplained… forehead… no relief… torture.

That's it—the Chinese Water Torture. Google responds quickly and explains the procedure in frighteningly descriptive terms. The purpose of water torture is to drive a person mad.

I search further and read the Wikipedia archive gaining a lot of knowledge. Houdini gave it that Chinese name in 1910 to add exotic mystery to one of his escape acts. That's a small comfort. Hippolytus De Marsillus initiated it in Medieval Italy for torture to be used by the Medici and the Church. Observing that repeated drops of water could erode stone, he thought the same thing would happen to the human body. So, what, he's been dead for centuries. I'm alive, and it's happening to me now. It's… it's… it's not happening… now.

Suddenly, the drops have stopped, I think. I wait, keeping my breath locked in my chest. I read further that contemporary research indicates that it was the restraint of the victim, not the dripping water, that caused severe anxiety and discomfort. And I am unbound from my imagination.

Several minutes have passed without a drop. I exhale deeply, letting my shoulders relax. I touch my forehead, and it's dry. I massage that spot with one finger looking for an indentation and smooth the skin in small circles, releasing the tension. I stop and wait, not twitching a muscle. Afraid the slightest movement might cause it to start again.

It's darker now. The sun has sunk low in the west, only a slowly diminishing fireball falling into the Gulf to sleep until another day. The slight breeze has stopped, the palms are still. I let down the window, and fresh air floods the interior.

I turn the key, and the engine starts. I press the accelerator, and the red tachometer needle swings upright, standing at attention. I turn on the radio, loud. I shout, and I sing. I have no more drops drilling onto my skull into my brain.

I know all about it now. I know the facts and fantasies. The history and the legends. I shift into drive and head home, secure in the thought that I have beaten this unexplained phenomenon, this illusion. Google has saved me and taught me a lesson.

Knowledge is power.

Ed N. White

A writer of mysteries. A teller of tales. Ed N. White lives on the Suncoast of Florida, writing about anything of interest. His Middle-Grade mystery, *Miss Demeanor, Teen Girl Detective*, by Celia J., will be published by Histria Books, LLC, in 2021.

FLORIDA YOUTH WRITERS PROGRAM

CREATE AN ILLUSION

FLORIDA WRITERS ASSOCIATION
YOUTH COLLECTION,

VOLUME 7

1st Place: The World Beneath The Waves

The sun shines on the ocean top
Like a jar lid whose bottom never stops.

Beneath the sea, octopi in disguise
Blend in like sparkles in the sky.

Leafy seadragon is hard to spot
Predators don't know if he's there or not.

Humans think the earth is so grand
But only a third is covered in land.

Next time you throw trash everywhere
Remember, another world is down there.

Lincoln Silverio

Lincoln wants to be a Marine Biologist when he grows up. His hobbies include scuba diving and video games such as Rocket League, Fortnite, and Minecraft.

Youth Writers Program
Florida Writers Association

2ND PLACE: BEAUTIFUL WORLD

Good morning, beautiful world
As I smell the crisp morning air
Good morning, amazing world
So green, I can't believe it
Birds singing softly
Dolphins talking in water

Good morning, beautiful world
So sweet and so fair

What has happened to my world?
The grass so brown, like ashes
Where are my dolphins, my birds
Where is my beautiful world?
So sweet and so fair
Was it all an illusion?

This isn't fair

Secelia Henning

Secelia likes to write and draw in her spare time. She is currently writing a book called *The Dragons Cove*.

Youth Writers Program
Florida Writers Association

3RD PLACE: UNFORGETTABLE DREAM

There was a boy
Who lived an illusion
Heart full of confusion
Who once had a dream
But it was just a delusion

Dreams of a shadow
Stalked in darkness
Lived in his mind
Like the whirling of the wind
Of the eeriest kind

This was the end
He laid himself to sleep
The shadows lived on
In his mind
Forever

Daniel R. Creve-Coeur

Daniel is an intelligent and astute young man. He is a leader among his peers who loves God and strives to do good. He is an exemplary student who enjoys math and works hard at all subjects.

Youth Writers Program
Florida Writers Association

HONORABLE MENTION: WITHOUT MY GLASSES

Everything's blurry,
Why can't I see?
It's quite scary
people have no eyes.

All I see is colors
With lack of details.
The whiteboard
has unreadable lines.

Is it me
Or is someone over there?
It can't be
Being nearsighted is not fair.

Arianna Perez

Arianna likes singing and has started BMX racing. She doesn't like wearing glasses!

Youth Writers Program
Florida Writers Association

HONORABLE MENTION:
SHADOW MAN

There's a man
Stalking me at night
He watches
my every move
As he stands
near my window
Always silent
Like a tree
That never moves
He keeps me
up at night
Big breezes blow
Finally, I look
Out the window
It's a scarecrow!

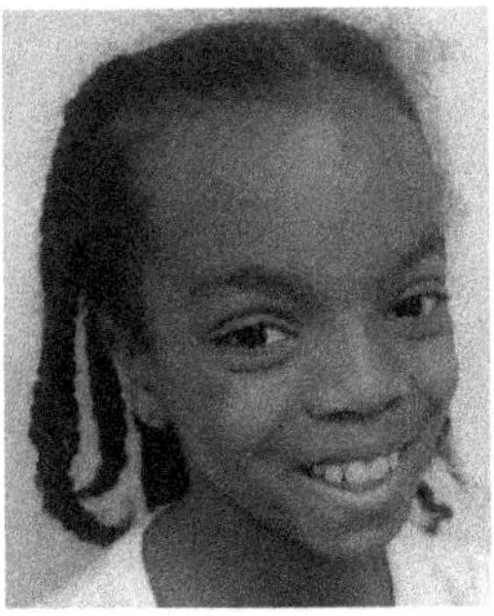

Ebelle Creve-Coeur

Ebelle is a talented, well-educated girl. She loves ballet and started dancing on pointe at an early age. Ebelle is a caring person with a soft personality yet is a strong competitor.

Youth Writers Program
Florida Writers Association

HONORABLE MENTION: FREAKED!

The buggy rocked slowly
like a phantom creeping across the floor.
At last,
Lewis arrived at his new home.
As he stepped,
rocks crunched under his feet.
Heart harshly beating,
a man standing by the door
Who gave him a pen and
left without saying a word?
Lewis heard noises
But now instead of rocks,
they were scary skeletons.
Heart racing,
He began writing
as if his life depended on it.
The painting on the wall stared at him
Suddenly, an abrupt jerk.
Lewis awoke, then froze
as if waiting for something,
anything to happen

At last,
Weird whirling wind
swirling storm
Door burst open and
Lewis disappeared
in a blitzing blink of an eye...

Nicole Collett

Nicole is an over-enthusiastic, bright, cheerful girl. She loves markers, pens, and any colorful writing utensils you give her. She is a great supporter and friend.

Youth Writers Program
Florida Writers Association

1ST PLACE: BLUE AND BLACK

She grabs the collar of her dress
Fastening every glass button
Before he comes home
Covering, covering, covering
Because maybe if she just covers up
No harm has been done
She buttons up
And sucks in every imperfection
Hiding her tears from the mirror
Because it saddens her to see the reflection
She's damaged goods
She has too many bruises
And is brought down by his eyes
Told she's not skinny enough
Told she's not pretty enough
Not worthy to be wrapped with a bow

She's buttoned up
Barely able to breathe
Because she's sucked in every breath
Pulled the dress so tightly
The buttons almost burst at the seams
It's a lovely dress
Blue and black
With gold thread woven through the back
It's a long sleeve
Floor length dress
With enough coverage to hide every blemish
She protects herself
And everything is held together by those delicate buttons
Because once her marks are covered up
They're not really there
They become an illusion
So when she has the dress on
Those buttons hold her together

Jacqueline Cook

Jacqueline Cook is an award-winning writer who enjoys writing very much, has been published several times, and attends Osceola County School For The Arts for creative writing.

Youth Writers Program

Florida Writers Association

2nd Place: Definition of Mortality

Broken and barren,
the life we have taken
is built upon the settlements
of illusions.
Yet we don't look back.
Hidden figures,
broken dreams,
deceased loved ones,
fall into our seams.
Shielded eyes
want to be blind.

Yet,
you must open your wounds
and let them see
that blood is a burden to carry.
Open your arms
reach out for love
that was never there.
And alone,
at last,
you finally feel
the side effects of knowing
you will never be whole.

Kazimir Reyes

Kaz is a high school student at University high school, he is currently part of the marching band, indoor percussion, and the vet tech program. He loves working with animals and playing music. He uses most of his spare time writing and editing his work.

Youth Writers Program
Florida Writers Association

3RD PLACE:
CLOUDS

Dog chasing a ball
Along comes the wind

Turtle tanning in the sun
Along comes the wind

Crab skittering on the beach
Along comes the wind

Dolphins swimming in the sea
Along comes the wind

Shape shifting menagerie sets them free
To become something new

My imagination is fueled
Along comes the wind

Sarah-Catherine Jackson

Sarah-Catherine is a unique girl who enjoys roller skating, playing with her dog and applying makeup. She has been a Girl Scout for many years and loves volunteering. Her favorite subject is Social Studies and her least favorite activity is reading books, but she loves writing utensils and stationery.

Youth Writers Program
Florida Writers Association

HONORABLE MENTION: THE FLAME WITHIN

The putrid scent of singed hair and charred flesh overwhelms me as I enter the small, windowless Birthroom. I feel ill but continue on anyway. The doctors always say that I will become accustomed to the smell, but I never have and probably never will. I have witnessed hundreds of Births, but the smell still unsettles me every time.

The Birthroom is dry; the ever-burning fire removes all traces of humidity from the air by early in the afternoon. As I cross the threshold, a woosh of dry heat engulfs me along with the acrid scent, creating a rather unpleasant experience. Everything about the Birth is.

When a Pyron is born, they are kept in the Birthroom for days. The first person they ever see, feel, and ignite is not their mother but a midwife like me. Midwives go through years of training to prepare for a Birth, but it never feels like enough. The first Birth they witness is always terrifying, as are the seven long months that follow while the Pyron learns control.

Pyrons are born with an uncontrollable flame. Their flame is battled, weakened, countered, and smothered for the first one-and-a-half decades with hours of studies and mindless activities. The first seven months of a Pyron's life are crucial to controlling its flame and it is the midwife's job to begin the over a decade long process to remove it.

I hardly remember my flame. It has been over four decades since it last danced across my palm, raced up my bare arms, and flowed through my heart. Sometimes I wake up from a deep sleep and feel a tingle in the pit of my stomach as if the last glowing embers of my flame stirred during my dreams. Once, not long after my second decade, I told my mother about the feeling. She looked down at me scornfully and told me to never speak of it again.

I never fully understood why our flames are a sin or why we can't keep them alive, carefully feeding them with our emotions and thoughts and growing with them as we develop. Why must they be stowed away and engulfed with anger until they are gone? Throughout my now almost six decades, I have asked this question many times. No one has ever answered. Why would they?

I have been told that I am ignorant and ungrateful for yearning to feel thc delicate lick of a flame against my heart. Pyrons say that the flame is a curse, a burden that needs to be contained by all means necessary. But the flame is part of us. I can feel a hole inside of me where it once danced. A gap that over the years has evolved into a deepening chasm, slowly chilling as I age.

The soon to be Mother is laying on a low fireproof table. Her hair is a deep shade of amber; the color shared by almost all Pryons. Her skin is slick with sweat and a hardened scowl is set like stone on her otherwise pleasant face. I, myself, have never given Birth, but I have witnessed more than enough to understand the entire process and to feel sympathetic for any Pyron who does.

The worst part of the Birth is the end. The Mother does not get to see or hold her newborn for seven tortuous months. They are left with an unsatisfied and heartbroken feeling after being separated from their child. I feel sorry for the Mother laying silently on the table. I always do.

It is not long before her child is Born. She is immediately wheeled out of the Birthroom in a rolling chair and her son is placed delicately into my arms. He has her amber hair and similar facial features. He has a small frame with delicate limbs attached. He has a raging flame.

I am dressed in the proper precautionary flameproof coat and wear goggles to protect my eyes, but in truth, I wish to feel the newborns flame. His palms are both alight with the uncontrollable fire and his veins pulse with a boiling liquid, snaking bright red lines along his pale skin. The doctors say that a flame is uncomfortable and dangerous for a child, but I disagree. The baby looks happy and content with the blaze hugging his torso and enveloping his fragile limbs. Nevertheless, I know it is my job to eradicate his flame.

I have done this before. I have taken care of many babies over my almost four decade long career. I have helped destroy the flame of more babies than I can count. Why then, is it so hard now? I know I need to begin the process to remove his flame, but the nameless baby boy rests so peacefully, with his head pressed against my bosom. His heart beats strong and steady against mine.

With a sigh, I reach for a book, the first of many I will read to him over the next seven months.

"One flame. Two flame. Red Flame. Blue flame. Bad flame. Bold flame. Evil flame. Old flame…" I stop. I can't bear to do this another time, to destroy a piece of another child. The little boy, whose eyes have yet to open, yawns, a tiny sound that warms my heart.

I feel something inside of me begin to stir. Hugging the baby tighter, I take off my goggles. It might be suicide, but I have an idea. I slowly shake off my protective coat and for the first time, touch a baby Pryon with my bare skin. To my surprise, I don't burn, instead, I am engulfed in a heavenly warmth.

The warmth begins outside of me and slowly works its way in. It reaches the last few glowing coals of my flame and reignites them. For the first time in over four decades, I feel alive. A bright fire nestles deep inside my heart and now I know that my flame will never be smothered again. I know that I will never suppress another child's fire. I know that everything I have ever learned is a lie. My flame is a part of me, not a curse. Not a parasite that needs to be destroyed. My flame is a blessing, a warm embrace. My flame is me.

I race out of the Birthroom, the baby burrowed deep in my arms. The Pyrons in the corridor stare at me and a few expectant Mothers begin to weep but no one moves. No one makes an effort to stop me as I violently rip off my name tag and throw it on the ground. Eve. It shatters and I scream.

"It is all a lie!" I don't wait for a response before I run. I exit the hospital without pausing. I know that I need to leave. There is no place for me here, in this cold, flameless city.

I take another look at the baby sleeping peacefully in my arms. Moses. Yes, that is his name.

Rachel Galpin

Rachel has lived in Florida her entire life. She became a published author in 2019 with the novel Saving Sand.

Youth Writers Program
Florida Writers Association

HONORABLE MENTION: FRIGHT NIGHT

Drone strike
People with fright
Bright light
Like a bad sight
Boom!
It ignites

A sleepless night
It wasn't right
People mourned
Some scorned
It was all because of
A satellite

David Creve-Coeur

David is an intelligent young man who dreams of becoming a civil rights lawyer and maybe even the first Haitian-American to become President of the United States of America. But for now, he enjoys attending SPARK and playing basketball.

Youth Writers Program
Florida Writers Association

FOOTPRINTS

FLORIDA WRITERS ASSOCIATION COLLECTION, VOLUME 12 AND FLORIDA WRITERS ASSOCIATION YOUTH COLLECTION, VOLUME 7

The theme for our next book in FWA's Collection series is *Footprints*. Florida Writers Association Collection, Volume 13, set to be published in the fall of 2021. It will include the youth collection contest, Volume 8, with the same theme.

Footprints could mean an area on a surface covered by something. Like a tire that makes a wide footprint, or the footprint of a laser beam, or the range of operation (as of a service)—a global footprint. Perhaps it's a marked effect, impression, or impact as in a footprint in the field of research? Maybe the track a hunter follows that turns out to be something else? Anything is possible. As always, fiction, nonfiction, essays (maximum: 1,200 words), and poetry (maximum 50 lines) are all eligible.

These short story contests, sponsored by the Board of Directors of Florida Writers Association, were created to offer our members an opportunity to be published, and another way to grow their writing skills.

Each year, the contest has a new theme. All writing must conform to that theme and must be within the total word limitations as set forth in the guidelines.

The annual contests are fun—they give you the opportunity to submit two entries. They stretch you, giving you parameters and guidelines within which you previously may not have considered writing.

All judging is done on a blind basis. Stories are posted by only title and number for the adult collection contest and by only title, number and author age for the youth collection contest. The number is assigned consecutively as stories are received. In the adult collection contest, judges read each entry entirely and evaluate according to how well it was written, was it strongly on theme, and did it strike a chord with them. Because the youth collection contest separates the entries into two age groups, judges also consider the writing-skill sets for each age group along with the same criteria as the adult contest. As with any judging, there is some subjectivity to the process. However, the judges understand that each entry selected as a winner must be ready for printing, as no editing is allowed after submission other than fixing minor typos that happen to be caught during the audit.

Next year is our fifth year for the Royal Palm Literary Award Competition Published Book of the Year winner as our Person of Renown for the collection book. This new concept is inspiring our members in their writing journeys and providing yet another way for members to become published authors.

As in the past, our Person of Renown will select their Top Ten Favorite entries out of the judges' top sixty only in the adult collection contest. The youth contest winners are determined by highest scoring judges' total…and we'll be off and running with another book for the Collection, and, another set of contests to look forward to for the following year.

ABOUT DARKWATER SYNDICATE

We are Darkwater Syndicate. We're the publishing company with a defense contractor's name, and that sums up our approach to books. Our mission is to be your source for uncommonly good reading.

We refuse to be mainstream. Our authors are not afraid to push boundaries and buck trends. Pick up one of our books and see why we call them "uncommonly good" reading.

We are headquartered in Miami Lakes, Florida.

Join us on Patreon.

Visit us at www.DarkwaterSyndicate.com.

Follow us on Facebook and Twitter.

CPSIA information can be obtained
at www.ICGtesting.com
Printed in the USA
FSHW021353250920

9 781946 378477